Buying this book or downloading it you donate 50 cents to the IHP association for the health and the safety of all the mistreated horses:

http://www.horseprotection.it

On their side

Humans don't always learn easily what respect for life is. They don't consider other animals as companions with which to cohabit, but like things to use and throw away afterwards. Horses, more than other species, suffer from this culture, which has little that is natural and a lot that is anthropocentric. A horse is hardly considered a friend, because he is always a horse "to do something": trotting horse, racing horse, jumping horse, dressage horse, riding school horse, carriage horse, circus horse…slaughtering horse: the same terminology underlines that he doesn't exist as an individual in the average consideration, but only on his utility. He doesn't have rights. IHP was born to encourage a change and to shake consciences: it is our solemn commitment to equines, who make us better persons with their gentleness, their depth and their pride.

THANKS!

A dressmaker
at the court of Versailles

Translated by Cristina Contilli

www.cristinacontilli.ilcannocchiale.it

Samanta Catastini

The nobility of spirit must not be measured with aristocratic titles.

Samanta

I dedicate this book to Francesco Barcelloni Corte, Italian writer who emigrated to Argentina.

www.samilla.wordpress.com

www.catastinisamanta.ilcannocchiale.it

PARIS, 1749

Amelie narrows into the mantle and she hurried, cold air seems to pervade even the humble garment of wool. Around the noise of the wheels of carriages is deafening and the dark color of the sky portends an impending winter storm. Madame Rose will be eager to see her return to know the reaction of the Countess Vigny to receive your gown. Sewing was not her only job, in fact after the untimely death of Alexandra, she had offered to surrender to the noble couture customers. This task also allowed her to enjoy the beauty of their city. At the same time she reminded the saddest moments of her childhood when she helped the poor mother to mend clothes of the rich ladies. Hunger and poor sanitation had left her orphan at the age of fourteen, and, only thanks to the kindness of the most popular dressmaker in Paris, she had been able to enjoy a bed and a hot dish. She was a good student and she learned quickly the art of sewing. Just earlier this year, after twelve years of hard work began to draw models from all major areas ladies of the French nobility. Sometimes the evening before falling asleep in the back shop wearing some clothes designed by her and she dreamed of taking part in a grand ball at court. Tales of customers about the wonderful palace of Versailles intrigued beyond measure, hoping one day we can go for even a simple delivery. She had no illusions about that. She just comes into the Place Vendome directed towards tailoring La Belle Dame where the new girl, Annie, is diligently cleaning the window. "Good evening, Amelie are already back?" "Yes, I returned on foot to see a bit our beautiful city. Madame Rose is inside?" "Yes, she is serving the countess Chambery. She is waiting in glory for studying a model to measure". Annie was taken after the death of Alexandra, a young and inexperienced but very willing. They immediately order established a good relationship of friendship. They shared the same bed and the same food but they had distinct visions of life.

Annie hoped to become a member of the nobility and she would do anything to achieve this goal. Amelie knew with certainty that she could never enjoy these comforts her so far away from birth. "Oh, here's my good costume." Madame Rose approaches her and she takes her woolen cape dragging once the center of the beautiful oval room, where a large table is perched on a large amount of fine fabrics. Many drawings of patterns on the walls hip and two big yellow velvet sofas where customers could easily see just the clothes sewn. "Finally you arrived I was about to leave." The Countess Juliette Chambery addressed the impatient look that highlights her big green eyes. She takes off his hat and loosens her long hair blond. "Tell me, mademoiselle, do you have some idea of the fabric to use?" "The most beautiful fabric. I want to be bright for the Opera Ball." Amélie was intrigued by the event but, for her professionalism and for love of her craft, she is limited to examining the material spread on the table without any questions. "This pink silk embroidered with gold flowers just arrived and it's really an extreme fineness. We could enrich it with lace to match, then your beauty will do the rest."

1.

"Monsieur Lavois want to see the king to ask some advice about the play of Moliere's Tartuffe." The Count Pierre supports the glass of champagne on silver platter at the center of the table, he gets up, gently settling the jacket of black velvet lined silver salutes and the noble ladies sitting on either side. The Baroness Tramèrie complacent smiles. "We expect to continue our discussion should resume tomorrow night or during the dance at the Opera?" "That depends on the needs of our beloved sovereign." Bows of courtesy before joining the server to the rooms of the king. His reputation with women made him famous not only at court but also in Paris. There was a young girl or lady already married not dreamed one night of love with him. Sure of his beauty he made a good use of this quality to obtain an excellent position in court. When the King Louis XV had discovered his eccentric way of dressing also due to his innovative taste about the predilection of the best French fabrics in circulation, had hired him as an adviser in the personal choice of clothing. So he had secured a comfortable apartment in the palace of Versailles and a comfortable standard of living considerably. Tall, dark hair and eyes blacks, stubbornly refused to wear wigs, like all the other courtiers, and, thanks to his tight clothes he displayed a very athletic and powerful. When, compliant crossing the Hall of Mirrors, he admires his figure reflected. Arrived in front of the royal apartments, the waiter, after knocking, opened the heavy wooden door inlaid with white gold. The king is waiting for him sitting behind his big desk full of papers and books. Cape lined with fur his figure, always set, he seems more impressive than usual. "Hello, my lord, what I owe the honor of this invitation?" "Oh, count Lavois, there I was just waiting." He gets up and he nods to Pierre to sit on the large sofa in red velvet. "Do you want a chocolate?" "With pleasure." In his eyes the waiter hands him a steaming cup and then he leale them with a bow. "Be aware of the future theater of Moliere's Tartuffe here in court?" Lately, they don't talk much. Everyone seems intrigued by this event. " Louis XV turned away to gaze out the large window of the room. "Madame de Pompadour always manages to amaze me. She loves acting and she involved in this representation many nobles. I enjoy seeing her so excited in preparing for this event so dear to her." The king had not even spared no expense to please her lover, while his wife, Maria Leszczynska, pretended not to notice the obvious love affair. "I suppose that the representation will be open to a few guests. "A very small circle including you, dear Count Lavois and I would like that you bought my dress for that night. Now you know my measurements and you have much better taste than me doing it." Pierre smiled in his heart he was already certain of that request and he felt proud of this task that was the envy of many other courtiers. "It will be an honor for me! If I may show you an alternative to our usual tailor in court, I have just been informed of a new Parisian costume very clever. She seems that work at the boutique “La Belle Dame” and she has a taste and sophistication unrivaled.” At these words the king leaves the window and he sit back to his imposing desk. Indulges heavily in the very back of the seat embroidered velvet and he smiled, amused. "A nice idea. Count, you always managed to amaze me. We try to bring a touch of novelty to Versailles!"

2.

"Amelie, these clothes are beautiful." Madame Rose had just come out after she closed her boutique. Annie had been precipitated in the back with just two dresses sewn. "What are you doing? Return immediately to the study. I don’t think that it’s the case to play to do the noble women, we're too big to act like two silly naughty." She rubs her hands in front of the burning road, and with a wooden spoon, she turns the soup, trying to avoid the gaze of tempting new roommate. "But, I don't propose to play! Indeed... We are wearing these clothes and we are going to the Opera Ball." Amelie turns suddenly clenching her fists against the sides. "What are you saying? Are you dreaming?" "Sometimes I dream. You don't want to spend your whole life sewing clothes for others and give up the healthy fun?" "Wear clothes rich and go to a dance of the aristocracy it seem fun within our reach? Come on, Annie sit that dinner is ready." "I don't think either! I take the blue and I dress my hair with a ribbon colored red and you grant that will help you to do the same with your hair." Amelie doesn't have the time to fight back because she has already taken off her clothes for wearing the sumptuous dress just chosen. "Stop! Madame Rose will kill us when she will come to know." Annie makes a face at first then she looks at the large mirror framed in gold. "Who should tell? Nobody will recognize. Just put a black mask in front of the eyes to go unnoticed." In a split second she thinks back to her sad childhood when she often dreamed of being able to attend a social event, just to see how they live "other," the rich. She spent the rest of her life working, enjoying her walks towns as the only moment of relaxation in a life devoted to duty. Why not get involved in this carefree night flight? Ultimately it is only one evening. Tomorrow she will resume her life with a carefree but always she will remember to keep her company in the saddest moments. She puts the lid on the pot, removing the apron and she takes a big smile. "Okay. I believe (to) you! But we're going to this dance only if you promise not to ever take off the mask and not to leave without my consent." "If I find that a prince who wants to kidnap me and he take me to live in his castle not even think twice to answer for him, even without your permission damned." "In that case I can be quiet. Miracles rarely happen." Before putting on her latest creation sartorial, she stops at the center of the study for a visit. The red fabric apparel is adorned with beautiful silver embroidery, the bodice has colored ribbons that are woven throughout its length, forming a large bow that adorns the heart-shaped neckline. The color is fully suitable to her hair and her complexion blacks diaphanous enlivened by her big green eyes. "Amelie how think if we will use these feathers for our hair?" “At this point we're really two noblewomen! And why not? Now we carry out this dangerous game." Immediately after the sentence she is surprised at herself, her life had never ventured much. And in looking in the mirror she is sure to have never been so beautiful.

3.

“Pierre are you giving to move? Just don’t wear any jacket will definitely sober." The Marquis Charles Pombery is sitting in the comfortable green velvet chair and he watchs the count, indecisive as always, is by reviewing their own clothes. "You talk so fast because you only go to the damn ball full of geese ready to jump to your feet." "Actually the opposite always happens and you know very well, it's useless to pretend not to see them." Pierre finally decides to a bell-shaped burgundy jacket with trimmings of gold, black vest and a white shirt with a huge lace neck. The velvet trousers of the same color to come to the knee leaving a show of beautiful white silk stockings and began to complete the eccentric dress with beautiful shoes with gold buckles. "Here I would say that so you can easily go unnoticed." The Marquis stands up and he nods to the servant to prepare the coach. When, passing through the rooms of the palace of Versailles, he strikes the silence that accompanies his steps. All other aristocrats have already directed to the Opera. It will be a lovely evening of intimacy for the king and for Madame de Pompadour, for once relieved of their duties as hosts. He arrived in the yard, the driver opens the door for him and he helps him to rise. "My dear, I know that tonight you can not help dancing with the Countess Chambery. Whenever you see rushes toward you with obvious enthusiasm of passion in his eyes." Pierre looks out the window and he admires the great avenues of the immense royal park. "I hope to avoid it. Tonight I want to hear speeches frivolous and empty." "Then you had to stay in your apartment and maybe to read a good book, because this lightweight women's dance is the host!" He fails to respond to his friend because, in his heart, he knows that he is absolutely right. Yet his rise at court was so fast because of his continuous visits to the various dances and social gatherings where the king had been able to appreciate his talents on fashion. That was his mask to try to save more than that to which he held, his ancient manor in Provence. When his father died the financial status of the family was very critical but for the world would sell its ancient castle. He was headed to Paris where he soon entered into the good graces of Louis XV and through his generous gifts he had started the restoration of the house. Fashion, textiles and the lightness of the court did not interest him at all but had to pretend with skill to accomplish his dream. "Oh, look at the crowd to enter. It seems that the city has poured to the Opera tonight! "The exclamation of astonishment Charles brings him back to reality suddenly. Indeed major access stairs are full of aristocrats with sumptuous clothes and hairstyles too. Pierre took his first woolen cape to greet the driver and he tells the exact time in which to take them back. Crossed the big front door the buzz is so strong that suffocate the same background music. Some noblewomen wearing black masks not to be recognized so they can flirt with more freedom. The huge central staircase is filled with people talking amiably with each other as you relish delicacies accompanied by good champagne. Charles where are you going?" "Oh, sorry my dear but I just saw the countess Deville. Do not miss me to see the multiplicity of ladies present." For some time the friend was trying to win the young lady but with little result. Actually he had to admit that was a rare beauty with her fiery red hair and her skin covered with freckles sexy. Maybe tonight the excitement of the dance can facilitate a more fruitful. Pierre is about to climb stairs when he sees a girl with dark hair and a striking red dress talking excitedly with the nearby companion. He can't see her because her eyes are hidden behind a mask of black silk. He still can't look away from her graceful figure. He walks toward her with a firm step without having the slightest idea of what to say just to make your acquaintance. He realizes that the girl has a slight jolt to see him come and leans slightly to his friend's shoulder, as a request for support. The ride never seems to end there are many people who stop to say hello or just to shake his hand. His close friendship with King made him a famous and competitive person. Surely all these honors intrigued by the mysterious girl or perhaps may even frighten. The closer the better known her pretty movements that do not hide their incomprehensible loss. He looks around several times as if that environment was the most magnificent stranger. "Good evening, Mademoiselle, can I have the pleasure of a dance?" It 's impossible not to notice the redness buying of her cheeks. It almost seems that the template serves only to hide and not as stupid excuse to flirt with several gentlemen present. "Good evening, I am very honored for your kind request, but..." Pierre didn't have the time to listen to the end of this sentence because the girl at her side asserting himself forcefully. "Monsieur my friend is very shy but I'm sure will be happy to dance with you, but, we can know your name?" "I am the Count Pierre Lavois mademoiselles and you?" "My name is Annie and she is my cousin Amelie. Of course we prefer to keep quiet for security our family." Amelie jerks and she blows her cousin with a look of anger. "Don't worry that I will not try to know more about you, provided of course that I have this dance." Cornered the smiles and holds out his hand to be accompanied at the center of the room. The journey continues in perfect silence while facing many noblewomen who observe them as they passed urgently.

This makes the girl stiffen Amelie who, perhaps unwittingly, holds his arm with more force. The large chandeliers lit with white candles warm the environment and create a play of shadows on the walls decorated with stucco. Kindly let the girl in front positions to start dancing. He feels his heart pounding against his chest and his breathing seems a little shorter. "We like to dance?" "Yes, but I don't dance very often. Forgive me if I'm not an expert but I don't like to attend the receptions." Pierre has the impression that in pronouncing this sentence is as free of a burden because suddenly close the hand is loosened and the cheeks lose their initial flush. He seems a bit more comfortable though not always intent on lowering the curtain of confidentiality between them. "I can't even ask if you attended the court?" "I just said that I don't love the holidays." Her cold response doesn't match the warmth of her voice." I had occasion to meet again because I understand not only your name. She smiles and she looks down before speaking again. "I live in Paris so I will not be difficult to meet again." "But I spend much time at Versailles... because this is where I live." "In that case I'm happy for you but I never had the honor nor the desire to visit the palace and I don't want to do in the future. I'm sorry but I think after this we should say goodbye nice dance!" In her big green eyes Pierre imagined the endless expanses of grassland in Provence where dreams of returning soon. Even the fresh scent of lavender brings him back to his happy childhood. "I have a tenacious character. I know this is not to your liking but I will do anything to meet you again and..." The music ends suddenly and Amelie has such a violent shudder at seeing near Pierre the Countess Juliette Chambery. "My dear, there I was looking for a long time." When you first time to meet with mock gallantry, she leaves her arm and she walks away quickly without looking back. "Wait..." The countess holds him taking his hand. "I interrupted something nice?" Instantly he realizes that would be futile to run after her, such was his haste to flee, his reckless behavior would also points out to malevolent speech. "No, you haven't absolutely disturbed. Would you like a glass of champagne?" "Willingly, taste it in your company will be a pleasure."

4.

When she reached Annie she was a feat to convince her to abandon the Opera. She was talking, or rather shamelessly flirting with a marquis, named Charles Pombery. Yet she had to leave as soon as possible not to see again that the Count was greatly disturbed. Moreover, if the countess Juliette Chambery had recognized them, she would certainly tell everything to Madame Rose. She could not afford to miss her work that the roof to sleep under. Annie sitting in the carriage was so furious not to talk to her and she looked badly. Amelie, had moved the velvet curtain to observe the city from the window, thinking that she had felt in the arms of the count. She knew that she would never have crossed the gates of Versailles and had to forget as soon as possible. Yet she understood that the emotion triggered by his proximity could not only be uncomfortable for women. "I don't understand because you wanted to leave the party so soon! I began to enjoy myself and you ruined it taking away without even a valid explanation." Try to keep calm even if your first instinct would be to slap her and blame her for the behavior showed that surface with a stranger. "I crossed the countess Chambery and I felt that I had recognized." "But if you wore the mask as she could recognize you?" "What do you think when you will not notice the tailoring of clothes hanging from the ones we wear tonight?" Annie looks puzzled, she seems to regret the situation they are hunted. "We could throw away to avoid suspicion." Amelie can't believe to her ears. "Are you kidding that is a week working day and night to achieve... but I try to readjust." "Of course! It's a good idea!" That was a genius found he had no doubt the problem was able to do before the next morning. Not only for the fatigue of the evening but also the complete lack of inspiration. Yet they would not find another way out to hide their stunt.

5.

Pierre thinks that he heard a knock but he is not quite sure. His head that bursts and swollen eyes from a sleepless night. Bedside last tasted champagne before going to bed, next on velvet chair, clothes the night before visibly crumpled. He doesn't remember how he managed to undress on his drunkenness. Having danced with the mysterious girl, Amelia, he was condemned to be able to find her, while also exploring the hidden parts of the operation but there is no trace of her. Then he pretended interest in the empty speeches of the Countess Chambery before vanishing without saying goodbye acquaintances. He had never returned from a party so early, nor was he ever managed to get drunk in solitude in his sumptuous apartment. "Pierre let me or wallpaper the door! Would this not be very happy our sovereign." Charles shouting in the corridor without worrying about pedestrians. He stands up leaning to the bedposts and he puts on his robe before opening his friend. "You're always better educated." "Mommy I do! But what did you do last night? You left me alone without even warning me that you went." Charles nods to sit down and he calls an attendant to be served hot tea with pastries to chocolate. "I was bored with the usual people and their tedious speeches." He takes a cookie and he leaves against the great back in his chair. "I thought that you had escaped with the Countess Chambery but then I saw her talking to other noblewomen while even the shadow of yourself." "It was... but fled from her!" The Marquis started laughing heartily. "It would be very happy with Louis XV, since want to give it to you in marriage." "I do not really want to ruin my life happy my sovereign." He takes the cup from the tray in silver and drinking tea all in one mouthful, its warmth seems to remove that annoying circle the head. "You can not deny that it is a creature of a striking beauty. Many men courting relentlessly but she only has eyes for you." Starts to rain furiously against the large windows provides the valet to light candles for the sudden disappearance of the weak sunlight. "I don't care if you don't have the beauty topics to share." "Since you've become so intellectual?" Pierre gets up and moves the long curtains of red velvet brocade, the gardens of the palace did not lose their charm even in the pouring rain. "Always, only that I'm not going to show it in public." "Look what a nice discovery I made today! And those two bottles of champagne? I want to believe that they have been drinking in solitude? "The persistent claims of the friend they're annoying than it should try to remain calm but not to lapse into vulgarity minutes. "Think what you want! I don't think the duty of explanation to anyone. " The valet beat feet to highlight its presence. "Excuse me count Lavois but the king has just expressed his desire to see you in private!" Charles smiles as he takes a pastry covered with chocolate. "I hope for you that the countess had not gone Chambery from her majesty to complain about your behavior." Pierre stands up and he throws his robe on the bed telling the footman who take to the dress." The idea doesn't worry (for) me. The king at the moment is too busy to please Madame de Pompadour to cure even the whims of other noblewomen.

6.

Amelie is breathing a sigh of relief to hear Madame Rose come just when they have just hung the last dress sewing. Of the two worn the night before had made four decomposing the bodices and skirts by inventing new creations. All the result of a sleepless night already full of emotion hitherto unknown to her and considered quite dangerous. In fact he did not know what love was but for the first time he heard the heartbeat suddenly increased their normal course. For this he decided to escape, was not accustomed to accept what had no rational explanation. Also felt out of place among all those noble intent to have fun so rampant. That game had not enjoyed even made her realize how great the social gap that separated her from the life of your dreams. Immersed in his thoughts did not hear Annie enter the studio to place a large vase full of red roses. "Hey, we did a great job, these clothes are more beautiful than before." Amelie smiles and rubs his eyes bloodshot with fatigue. "Good, you had the foresight to go and buy flowers. Apparently everything in its place. " At that moment Madame Rose enters with a firm step and fast, like every morning. "Hello girls! That smell good and beautiful roses. You have already cleaned everything and also bought the flowers. What gems you are! "Laid his cloak of wool on the couch and stops to admire the four dresses hanging. "But how wonderful. And where these came from? "Before watching Annie begins to babble in confusion. Amelie runs immediately to his aid. "I spent the night to show her how to sew a dress noblewomen. Sooner or later you must learn the job and I can tell who the real talent. " "Brave were making progress and I see that you have established a good relationship. I'm happy. " Then he turns back to the hanger and looks puzzled. "Amelie but your last two creations?" Annie opens her eyes and she nods to let her speak. “I did propose to create four of them to use because the fabrics were so precious that it seems wasted for only two dresses. He spent a minute in complete silence that seems like an eternity. Madame Rose then turns and smiles of taste. "Good, Do you understand what is necessary to make the most of our raw materials," The girls heave a sigh of relief and prepare to spend a new long day at work.

7.

The groom is a sign for Pierre to follow the highest floors of the palace. He did not take long to realize that is accompanying him in private apartments of Madame de Pompadour. He still prefer not to ask questions because he knows that the boy would not know what to say, after all is only running a real command. A waitress is waiting for them at the entrance. He bows and he dismisses his colleague with a smile. Then mention to Pierre to follow along a narrow corridor before opening the door of the king's favorite. A large painting immediately attracts your attention. It's the famous portrait depicting an attractive madame De Pompadour which her gaze is turned to the viewer, the darkness behind him emphasizes his translucent skin and her large dark eyes. "Hello, Count Lavois that pleasure is to see you again!" The soft voice of the Marchioness welcomes him into her apartment while the king, who sits on a chair in complete calm, smiles, raising an arm in salute. The scent of countless flowers pervades the room. The waitress hands him a chair upholstered in red velvet in order to accommodate their presence. Pierre first bows and then sits without showing the slightest awe. "The pleasure is mine Marquise de Pompadour and also a great honor to be received in your rooms." Louis XV bursts into laughter. "We try count! We know how popular you are in winning the women. Your reputation goes before you!" "I could never do such a thing! At least you now!" "You are a hopeless villain." The Marquise offers him a cup of steaming tea and she shows him a silver tray full of pastries. She has a small stature but she has a unparalleled elegance. Dark eyes, bright, attentive and above all intelligent. Brown hair often tied back in two long braids. Pale complexion with porcelain skin, smooth, without any defect or imperfection. A nose commensurate with the oval face enlivened by fleshy lips. Yet the king was seized from his most profound education and education than its apparent physical attractiveness. "Enjoy these fabulous chocolate chip cookies because it seems a bit out of sorts. Or am I wrong count? "No, king, I spent a sleepless night. Last night I must have eaten something rotten and I could not sleep for the tummy which I emerged." He is surprising before himself for the choice to lie but his appearance should not be the best, perhaps Charles was not joking when they had pointed out a few minutes before. "I never thought that you were so sensitive in stomach. In any case not detain you much because I have found the seamstress you talk." Pierre tries to do much was his last interview with Louis XV and he remembers to have mentioned the famous Parisian couture that lately is sweeping all the court ladies. The Marquise sips his tea and then he sits in front. "Yes Mademoiselle was not difficult because he speaks so well with Chambery as intrigue anyone. Taylor also completed our court is very repetitive and I know that this boutique works a clever young girl in designing and sewing patterns including the latest fashion." The king gets up to make a new cake, then he puts a hand on the shoulders of the Marquise. "I've already done the creative convene tomorrow afternoon in the apartments of our dear Phillip and I wish you were there to help in the choice of fabrics. I recommend you try to sleep well tonight, I want that you are in perfect shape. "

8.

Amelie tries to concentrate on designing a new dress as a man but her head pounding incessantly. Fatigue is presenting the bill. The morning was well spent because thanks to the arrival of new fabrics had a lot of work to arrange and catalog them. Annie helped her by cutting off small pieces to be affixed to the sample. They no longer spoke the night before because Madame Rose watched carefully while tidying the study. Since the early afternoon, hopes that does not enter anyone to order a dress because it seems to be short of ideas. "I can't believe it! O my lord!" The voice startled startles the mistress of the chairs, but they get up to go see what happened. They look worried, terrified by the idea that it may have found their escape by night. Then opens the study door and puts his hand to his heart. "There is a royal carriage out and the driver just opened the door ... A girl is coming here in my shop. Hurry, hurry, get up and get ready to bow to the new customer. " Annie appears in seventh heaven, the very idea of seeing any noble court makes daydreaming. Amelie finds himself confused do not know whether to be happy or upset. Count Lavois the night before had never asked if it happened at Versailles because he lives there. This was enough to make it even more nervous than the fear of not being good enough for the work will be commissioned. Close the door and hear the voice of Madame Rose agitated trying to meet the newcomer." The Girls is the Baroness Marie Tramèr that has failed to bring a letter of His Majesty Louis XV." Both bow. "We are honored to meet you!" She has the long red hair that falls behind, very fair skin and big green eyes. There seems to be at ease because you look around before you open your mouth insistently. "I came at the request of King that he would like to receive the young costume to court to commission some clothes for the Marquise de Pompadour." Amelie is petrified by the wonder years, while a slight push to encourage her to speak. Fortunately Madame Rose opens her mouth and she breaks the embarrassing silence that it was created in the study. "But it will certainly be a pleasure to work for a lady so famous for our beloved sovereign." Meanwhile, the Baroness is touching some clothes on display. "Well in that case tomorrow at three o'clock a carriage will pick you up. Take care to bring more samples can and most fashionable clothes at this time. If you have talent as they say, all the courtiers will compete to get your clothes!" Amelie smiles and immediately she thinks that night will really stand to look fresh as a daisy. It's not every day that you are in the presence of the king. Especially for a humble seamstress like her. And Versailles, from what she had told, it’s so great that it will be virtually impossible to encounter the beautiful Count.

9.

"You were right count Lavois on that boutique, La Belle Dame, I could admire the fabrics of excellent quality." Baroness Tramèr him about moving his hands curled into the air. Once he found her irresistible and its superficiality had quickly tired. Did not deny his obvious physical attractiveness but she seemed a nice box empty. Among them was a report was lightning at the end of which were discovered more friends than before. He was aware that she could tell of daily life but not the innermost feelings. So he tended not to mention the pleasant encounter two nights earlier. He would have filled with embarrassing questions. Yet in two days had failed to discover anything more about her because it was not easy knowing only his first name. "I have spoken very highly of this costume but I never went to the boutique. But the countess Chambery clothes are really beautiful and very sophisticated." "You fell into his trap?" Absolutely not. It's a beautiful woman but I don't wish nor seek a wife nor mistress. " They were walking in the park of the Orangerie even if the winter temperature was not the best. Anyway walk put him in a good mood, if he remained in his apartment should have been listening to tedious speeches of Charles on his latest conquests. "My friend I see you a bit absent lately. There is something that upset you?" "Nothing important. Always the same concerns. I am a bit 'shaken to think of Madame de Pompadour had to help in choosing fabrics for your new wardrobe... Let's say that I almost fear of not being good enough. A bill is to choose another male clothes is to please a woman bred and refined as the marquise." Baroness stops the hand and take a look straight in the eye. "You taste to sell. Our king was right to call you into question." A simple phrase but so reassuring to hear it again to the occasion. "Thanks. You are always very kind." While they decide to take the way back to the palace a royal carriage stopped before the great gate of gold waiting for the pass.

10.

He heard so much about Versailles as to have no more idea how to imagine. The mere sight of the infinite deleted enamelled gold hits for the imposing but at the same time feel an intruder. The palace is so immense that they are unable to complete to admire. As the fantasy of Amelie had tried to recreate these architectural splendours never be able to reconstruct these in his mind. The carriage stops at the main entrance, where three valets, after helping her get the nod are to follow. One of them is responsible dell'ingombrante suitcase containing the sample. Try to simulate as best he can but wonder realizes admire his mouth open. Salt a large staircase and continues to follow the servants in complete silence. The route crossed many noble women who stop to look through the air curiously. It seems never to arrive at their destination are many who walk the corridors and stairs going up. Suddenly he stops in front of a beautiful white door with gold stucco. A maid opens it and invites them to enter. At this point, Amelie begins to tremble, to meet the famous mistress of King, the curious, not everyone's day. The atmosphere is warm, cozy and scented by the myriad of flowers scattered all rooms. A long hallway filled with chandeliers above the room from which more carefree voices. When entering the antechamber remains stunned for a moment. Would never have thought to find himself before him the king Louis XV himself. And the more she is smiling warmly. "Ah finally able to see this famous seamstress mentioned in town!" A female voice soft and gentle turns the shooting. Indeed such was the wonder of seeing their king not to have noticed that the woman is at her side. So thin and short stature to be almost overwhelmed by the figure of the sovereign. Of his person, mainly affects facial features, a perfect oval, translucent complexion, light brown hair tending to blond, big dark eyes and lips very fleshy. Her gaze expresses gentleness and understanding even before having exchanged a word. She wears a simple yellow dress embellished with colored embroidery. Neck a beautiful necklace of pearls and diamonds. "Sit down dear ... About what is your name?" "Amelie". She can not utter another remains as firm as a statue in the middle of the room while the groom puts his suitcase and leaves quietly. Louis XV bursts into laughter. "Girl do not worry! We never ate anyone! "He bows before her, so embarrassed, before sitting in the big red velvet chair that the waitress is holding out. "But that big suitcase! Do not tell me you brought all the fabrics of your boutique? "But some Marchesa for you this and more! I am truly honored to serve you and hope to achieve for you the best clothes in all of France. " "How cute you are! You almost make me move ... But this precious open casket are too curious. " The marchioness appears before a child a gift bag while the king calmly sipping a hot chocolate, very comfortable in his chair, enjoying the comedy scene. Amelie kneels and opens the leather bag that seems about to burst, acting almost on impulse not realizing that the door behind him has just opened to let in another guest. "Earl finally! I had almost lost hope of seeing you since you are always on time, you is not delayed ten minutes! "" Excuse me but the Baroness Tramèr Majesty asked me to accompany her in the park and I took advantage to take a pleasant stroll. I had not noticed the time. " "And when in the company of a woman is more than understandable. Come, sit beside me and give your field review! "Amelie has not yet raised its head, too busy in their choice of patterns to be exhibited but not so absorbed as not to notice the vague familiarity of the male voice. The hands begin to tremble slightly. Can not be him, Versailles is so great and can not be so intimate friend of the king to sit by his side. Everything is ready in his hands can not linger or find other excuses for not getting up. You see the corner of that man is already settled, known vaguely of beautiful black calf shoes with big bows in red velvet. The scent of lavender that give off his clothes and embracing and inviting. "This girl is the famous dressmaker we mentioned the other day.

His name... What I carelessly forgot the name. Forgive as you have said to call you? "Now duty calls, can not refuse an answer to the Marquise. Slowly raises his head before seeing beautiful black velvet pants and then a coat of the same color. "Amelie. My name is Amelie! "And the count before her, to her great surprise, it is the man with whom she had danced a few nights before. "But you are a girl..." By trying to rush immediately to speak of what is going to say. "No, I think you're wrong. You can not seen me before, except in the boutique where I work. " With a single glance, perhaps too severe, the Count seems to have immediately understood his fear of discovery and hence its loss of credibility. Embarrassed smiles while moving a cowlick from his face. "You are right. Excuse me I think I'm confused. " Then the king, in a friendly manner, unleashes a nudge to the side. "You are always the same rake. You know so many ladies to forget even their physical appearance, "blushes without taking his eyes off her. "Please majesty before so I do not paint a young woman." Fortunately, the Marquise breaks this debate almost grotesque. "Come with us count Lavois and let her work! The tissue samples Amelie has just deposed our promise on the table really well." The heat of the journey seems unbearable for a moment, she felts her throat dry and hands get wet with sweat. Then in a split second she thinks that she can ruin an opportunity like this only a vague romantic encounter lasted only minutes. Begins to describe the various patterns and show the material which is used to achieve them. Madame de Pompadour seems very indecisive because attracted to everything that is proposed. "Monsieur Pierre So what do you think give me more?" He approaches the table and gives Amelia a steaming cup of hot chocolate. But would reject such is the thirst and fatigue that welcomes. In taking his hand touches the hot and powerful. Has a slight shudder, imperceptible to the present. "Thanks. Very kind of you. " The waitress on her right, the young girl who had first opened the door, hands her some cookies from an elegant silver tray. He sits down and tastes a while the Count and the Marquise watch designs, caressing the cloth placed on the side. That little sweet bite awakens the mind and gives her the energy to finally break the ice and give vent to his creativity. "Prefer to live alone with basket or want something more simple?" The Count took the floor in his place. "I guess you could do both in a range like that for a bit 'you will not have to think but only to your wardrobe accessories and jewelry. The king, who by then had risen and was looking out the window, bursts into laughter. "Hey, Earl Lavois go there otherwise you will weaken plan my finances." "In what we think when we get to choose your wardrobe. At these words Amelie felt a strong dizzy but was able to simulate the malaise. Already remained difficult to believe that you can sew for the Marquise de Pompadour, let alone the king. The king waves his hand in the air and takes a white rose from a vase near. "I think that it's better to postpone this task! What I invent my personal tailor? "The count is close to a window to examine the color of some fabrics is so absorbed by not responding immediately to the king. Then he turned and, looking almost defiant, says Amelie intensely. "It means that I'll embarrass this promising seamstress!" The marchioness raised her head to one pattern and begins to laugh in a very composed. "Amelie Oh this is really a big problem for you! You are faced with one of the men most eccentric and demanding in terms of clothes in all of France! "Stand up, shaking their fists at his sides, which mitigates this anger welling up inside. "Every challenge is for me one more reason to grow in my work. So much the better! "Immediately after the sentence you look at the large mirror hanging in front of the large wooden table. The suit decided to wear is not the best. Certainly could not afford a dress big lady because it is only an ordinary working-visit to court. Even if she could sew a great opportunity for he preferred to wear simple clothes, no basket, with a very chaste and-neck with long sleeves embellished on their lapels, a light white lace. The fabric has the red and green flowers embroidered on a white background white. Hair rebels gathered under a clear cap and no necklace around his neck, since he had never possessed. The cheeks, both the heat of shame, are on fire but give it a nice color. Surely the count may not have any interest in a girl so unattractive and extremely pure. Blinks several times as if to remove these silly thoughts and to find the concentration needed to continue its work, the only reason why is in that wonderful palace. "I will recommend this wonderful amber silk on which I could put the red velvet at the seams to create a very strong play of color, which does not go unnoticed. "Sublime as an idea! The colors are so cool and the fabrics that I show are so soft to the touch." The Count Lavois unbuttons the coat from which emerges a beautiful white silk shirt, listen with interest your proposal for fashion. Amelie looks away from the man so sure of himself. "I could also add some red feathers along your neck and leave three to pin in your hair. Revive your beautiful brown hair!" The Marquise drinks a bit 'of his hot chocolate and then rises suddenly. "I am elated and curious to see this dress as soon as possible. Please take my measurements. I can not wait to wear your creation. What about Monsieur Pierre? "The count is playing with a button on his jacket thoughtfully at the request of Madame de Pompadour's face shot up as he was awakened with a start. "What is interesting and original idea. I would say the best thing is giving way to his talent because it seems that he has to sell! "Surprised by such a compliment given that until recently had donc everything to make things difficult. Hides the surprise and starts to write down the measurements on a blank page using the fine nib gold lying on the desk. "You have made me want to do well without any clothes basket. Say something less challenging to be able to wear for a hike in the countryside. " "This is beautiful! And when did you go to the country? Your walks are very long but here in the gardens of Versailles where every courtier waiting to see you put "The king mocks his mistress in jest and at the same time, very affectionate. She smiles lovingly and looks in the mirror in which is closely following the movements of Amelie undertaken to examine his figure. "Every lady follows my tastes so I could launch a more simple and sober fashion. I see nothing wrong. " The count is approaching with slow steps and rhythmic, like a soldier intent to implement the march just learned. He stops in front of the Marquise and takes her right hand to kiss. "You are much more discerning about what you want to show. Not only make it even more famous Madame Rose's shop here and this seamstress but also managed to inaugurate a new era of costume. " Amelie tries to keep the feet of Madame de Pompadour to finish its measurement and not cross again gaze quell'avvenente libertine. "It will be enough to wear a suit different from the usual fees to attract even more attention of courtesans. The fire crackling behind him seems to wrap up the heat to take your breath away. Try a way out with class and neglect, will not stay in that apartment for the rest of the afternoon. "Marquise if you allow me I have a proposal to make." She feels the eyes of the Count on her neck, she assumes an upright posture and she mades that conveys the confidence that is missing. "Tell me dear, I'm all ears." It's lime lips completely dry tension. "Since I have your measurements I beg to cucirvi basket with two dresses and two garments easier. I will take care to choose the best fabrics in my possession and enrich them with more decorations possible. I'll try to make unique pieces. " The king reached his favorite and sits beside him. "My dear, I would say that it really is a better solution, at least let freedom of expression to the fantasy of this young girl! True Count Lavois?" "Certainly, I think that it's the best choice." Amelie bows and collects fabrics and patterns scattered all over the table, the waitress helps to place them in his leather suitcase. At the drop of the Marquise, the door opens and enter the three servants who had an hour before the conduct in those sumptuous rooms. You leave with a big smile as the king presents his greetings to Madame Rose. "Let me accompany you to the carriage?" The

Count approaches air safe, while a valet takes your luggage just closed. "No, no trouble I think these guys are more than sufficient." She turns and heads toward the exit hastening the pace. Only when he made a few steps along the corridor feel the powerful voice of the king, who jokingly addressed to the beloved subject. "It's the first time I see a frightened young lady, usually fall at your feet with a single glance!"

11.

For the first time since his arrival to Versailles Pierre through the gallery of mirrors without gaze at. The unexpected encounter with the famous Parisian dressmaker has shocked and intrigued him at the same time. When he danced with her a few nights before, he had not the slightest doubt of her noble origins. But... Of course she had not been difficult to find a pretty dress to wear since she herself could have been sew. Yet her gestures, her safety dance and her confidentiality resembled more to a person of high rank that a girl of the people. Perhaps her constant contact with noblewomen, customers of the boutique La Belle Dame, had facilitated in her social formation. He is still absorbed in his thoughts when he opens the door to his apartment and he sees Charles lying on his four-poster bed complete with glass of champagne in hand. "Congratulations! What are you toasting? I hope you will be taken off your shoes before you throw on my silk sheets." Pierre throws his coat on the velvet chair and threw himself on the other by the fire. Check the bottle on the coffee table and then pours the last drops, now warm. "It's been along this workshop with our sovereign. I was almost asleep. " "I don’t recall invited to have you in my room." Charles gets up and sits the blue velvet jacket visibly crumpled. White wig with curls remains on the bed while her hair was all matted, falling over his face. The scene is so funny that both burst out laughing like two kids who have just combined a prank. "I know I'm a clown and not think of being in your room but I was bored to death and have come to find you. Then I found this full bottle and I could not resist." "This does not surprise me at all, you're a lover of excess is nothing new." The Marquis is trying to accommodate the hair gazing at the large mirror on the wall. "And you, however, you lose so much time behind the fashion. What a bore! "Pierre pity from the absurdity show, gets up and helps him to settle down. "I follow fashion but at least I refuse to wear those silly wigs. Then sit by the fire and after several minutes of silence, the count shake the bell to call a servant. "You can bring some cakes? Thank you." Charles studied the perplexed, his expression after the nice skirmish a few minutes earlier, he is once again dark and gloomy. "What's wrong? You don't seem friendly like all other days. " Count sighs about to open his mouth when the attendant comes back with a silver tray full of sweets. It lies on the table along with a steaming teapot. It takes a chocolate biscuit and after tasting it decides to respond to his friend. "Today I met the famous seamstress in all

Paris talking. Really talented, very polite and also very nice but... "I don't know if immediately reveal her true identity but can not even hide it sooner or later you might come across Charles in many corridors of the palace. "But what? You have a face look like a corpse! "And 'the girl with whom I danced last night at the Opera." The revelation stunned the Marquis but only for a few moments since then bursts into laughter. "Come on! She (Amelie) has deceived us as an experienced actor, I would suggest her to Madame de Pompadour of writing for one of her theater, " "No joke, please. How must I do now? I was going to ask for a dance, but a simple working class can not come to Versailles." "You could apply for a permit to the king. With the consent of anyone who may be in the palace!" The count gets up and shakes his fists against the sides. "Have you forgotten that the king wants to marry the Countess Chambery? Would never accept to see me with a girl of humble origins, even if it is the most famous seamstress in town! "Charles is struck by the anger of his friend. Stay calm, sitting on comfortable velvet chair, sipping his tea. Watch the count, smiling at him with affection. "But his favorite may make him do whatever he wants. And if this seamstress about how you say his name? " " Amelie." " Well, if that Amelie has conquered with her grace and she will do well with her creations, the gates of Versailles will be wide open."

12.

For all this travel Amelie was not able to close her eyes although she was exhausted. She could not realize what had just happened. She made the journey to Versailles imagining but after entering the apartments of Madame de Pompadour was no longer able to enjoy that luxury architecture. Indeed he had only hoped to get out of that golden palace as soon as possible. The sight of Count Lavois had taken my breath away and had increased his discomfort. Its sad thoughts stop immediately as you enter the Place Vendôme. The carriage stops at the boutiques, Amelie kindly greets the driver and heads inside, almost running. Annie opens the door and take the leather suitcase that lies just on the floor. "Well? What a tired face, but that happened to you?" " Madame Rose?"And she is in the studio with a client who came to pick a dress. Come on, you see before you capture and for news on the outcome of the visit to the king, tell me something. Do not make me stay on your toes!" Then you drop damask chair beside the door, dropped his head and squinting. "Versailles is a dream, much more beautiful than a person can imagine. Great, impressive, extremely luxurious and opulent. The magnificent gardens so they can not be told. The immense palace of Count Lavois find myself in the same apartment and the Marchioness of sovereign! "Annie looks at her with eyes wide open for a few seconds and is unable to speak. "But I can not believe! So is a close friend of the king?" "Unfortunately yes. In truth adviser in terms of morality. I thought that I would never see again... But! "Annie kneels at his feet and put your hands on his legs. "What a coincidence!

What luck to have a position so valuable, the envy of all! Did she courted?" Amelie looks incredulous when speaking without taking breath. The blocks are shaking hands in the air with theatrical emphasis as an actress. "Are you crazy? I am neither a noblewoman with a title to be attained nor with great beauty... What comes to your mind? Instead of worrying if I recognized and has revealed our silly stunt! You realize that if she finds Madame Rose, we find ourselves on the street within a few minutes?" " You always think the worst!" " No, I am a realist and dreams you too! Get up now! "Annie makes a disgusted face and only when standing start smoothing the folds of her skirt wool. It looks like a schoolgirl who can not speak for shame. Conduct not in keeping with his character since it is almost always verbose. "See also the Marquis Charles Pombery?" Amelie sprang from the chair jumped suddenly rediscovering the power lost. "If I slap your mother! But continue with these silly questions? First of all, is not our world, Put it right on the head. ... And then you think I made a tour of pleasure to know new friends? "Embarrassed and shocked by his reaction backwards a few steps. No time to open his mouth that Madame Rose falls like a fury in the anteroom of the study. "Girls were screaming thing? I have a major client does not seem the best way to accept it. " Both bow and turning a sorry sight. "Amelie, please join me in the studio. You greet the Countess Vigny because you asked several times". She takes the leather case and she entered with decision in the main room of the boutique. "Ah, good evening, dear. I've waited until now because I would ask you to dress a model. Waiting to see the latest trendy clothes." She lies the suitcase on the big table and she opens it while performing a big smile, hoping thus erasing all signs of his fatigue. "Here are all the latest news. If you find something you like ask and see what we can do together." Madame Rose's face relaxes contracted with rage, offering a chair to the countess. "Thanks. How would I do without you Amelie? All your creation inspires admiration. " I wonder if the count

Lavois, after seeing her clothes, will be the same idea. Better to drive this thought and throw himself into work. Because these days the young seamstress will have a good deal of trouble.

13.

"Today, despite the temperature there is really a beautiful sun. And it's more pleasant walk along the Grand Canal. If I had worn the cape with fur instead of wool that would have been warmer. Count? Monsieur Lavois, but do you not listen me?" Pierre is completely lost in thought for some minutes. He finds that it difficult to focus on the lightness that the countess still Chambery list unabated. He decided to accompany her to walk in the park of the palace only out of respect for the king but could not feel any attraction for the beautiful girl so much admired at court. "I'm sorry I was thinking that I have to sign some papers for my old possessions. Forgive me I was not very polite, I regret."

Juliette addresses a passionate look carefully tries to avoid watching the water slightly wavy channel. "Don't worry about thhis, count, surely you have your thoughts! How can I brighten your concerns?" Pierre turns and takes her right hand, wrapped in a soft leather glove, and after having kissed the smiles gently. "It's just your presence to relieve any pain. Please lay on my arm to continue this walk." Only after consulting the body of the Countess surrender against his right shoulder, cursing himself for having made this false claim. She felt she had no choice, tell her the truth would only embarrassed his relationship with the King. This takes away the breath but the price to pay to save his land. If Louis XV did not repudiate other revenue to pay off debts incurred by his father. Yet must find a way out of this mess, paradoxically would like to marry a woman for whom proof attraction and passion. Until yesterday he was confident he had not yet experienced this feeling yet the mere sight of Amelie's heart was startled. She had initially blamed the momentary regret at having discovered his real position in society but then the thrill had continued to haunt him every time he met her gaze. Her usual sunny disposition had given way to one side more gruff and taciturn. Initially she had seemed so helpless then, after having met the Marquise, his bearing had started to express an iron dignity. In his eyes she read a commendable pride in their work. Perhaps it is no coincidence that all Paris praised his qualities as a costume designer. A distance of twenty-four hours did not yet give a name to this confusion that his presence had created in his heart and his mind. Suddenly the sound of horses galloping him back to reality and only then realize that you once again distracted by talk of the countess. "Hello, Count Lavois!" The King Louis XV stands beside them as they followed his number remains at a safe distance. "Sir, good morning to you!" Pierre bows for a moment leaving the arm of her companion. "I am pleased that you invited Madame Chambery to make a pleasant walk. It 's a real joy for me to see you together." The King never fails to emphasize his hope for their future marriage. Countess belongs to one of the families and dearest to him for the count should be a great honor to be able to ask for her hand. If only he knew that instead Pierre every day thinking about how to avoid this duty. "Count you look tonight in my apartment. Invite also your friend, the Marquis Pombery. Enjoy a fantastic dinner venison just caught. " "Of course I will!" The horse takes the gallop, followed by royal guards and noble love of hunting. "What luck! How many courtiers would like this invitation. You have bewitched so much preferable to other aristocrats with ancient origins. Pierre again offers his arm to the countess who is looking at him with languid eyes. "I did not do anything to obtain it!" "But what little you did was more than enough. And I can not hide that your charm is very intriguing because you do nothing to highlight. Better not answer that sweet flattery in order to avoid further misunderstandings. His every word is interpreted as a possible declaration of love. Only because that's what Madame Chambery has been waiting for. "I think that it's better to include the sky became threatening and the thought of having to attend a dinner of game puts me in a bad mood. I hate meat!" This is not an excuse but the truth amazed.

14.

Amelie is sewing tirelessly for over two hours when a knock on the door. Annie has just gone out to buy fresh flowers and Madame Rose, however, has been invited to the home of Marquise Mercaille. You just have to lay the red silk on the table and she opens the score. To her great surprise she finds herself in front of a man and not any one but the Count Lavois himself. "What are you doing here?" But what a nice welcome! You want me to stay on the street? It isn't so hot, we're still in January and I think that soon will also begin to rain." Behind him there is no real car but a beautiful black horse neighing in their direction. The Count realizes his surprise and he indicates the faithful companion. "I came with my better half is called Altoprato, I hope you don’t mind." Dazed and confused she moves to let him pass. The woolen cape that wraps releases a fresh scent of lavender. For a moment, cursing the fact that one does not know what to do its proximity makes it so scary. "Please sit in the studio, or rather in the study and forgive the confusion but I was just fabricating a dress for the Marquise de Pompadour." "I regret having lost. Are you alone?" He shows the velvet chair to sit and approaches the silver tray to take a plate full of biscuits. "Madame Rose is at the hoouse of a customer and Annie is just out for shopping. If you wait a moment go to the kitchen to heat water for tea offer. Count the smiles and he starts to browse the clothes hanging. The journey to get in the back room seems endless, even if it is within walking distance. Dare not even imagine what drove him to get up there. When part of the study surprised him to see some of his patterns. "We have designed this you?" "Yes, it's my job." She takes one of the best served in china cups and pour the steaming tea.

"Don't be afraid I did not come to check your work by the king but I was anxious to see you." Lower your eyes to hide his embarrassment. "Sorry, but I don't understand you. I don't believe to be so interesting after all are only a seamstress! If you refer to the Opera Ball I must admit it was just a stupid stunt. And I'm sure that will never happen again." Monsieur Lavois starts to laugh before you approach her and take her right hand. Amelie takes it a shot. "What do you fear? There do anything wrong. You have my word. I was curious to see you because I was captivated by your appearance but even more from your behavior. Proud and calm at the same time. Your eyes reveal a pure and generous... "Do not let him finish, he gets up and turns away. " The count does not live in the world of fairy tales. You live in Versailles, you know very well the king and the Marquise de Pompadour. I'm just a commoner who had the fortune to enter the palace, but only for work. Please do not continue to insult. I can never be part of the world, can only serve you!" He hears the sound of the cup resting on the table. "This means that you too have felt something for me. Otherwise you would not have done this careful analysis of the situation but let me give you..." "Must not go, take your cape and go away before it starts to rain. I would be grateful if it came back again. It 'best to not see us both. Actually belong to two completely opposite! "He can not turn while the Count collects his things. "Okay I'm going. But I assure you does not end here. Throughout my life I have never felt what I felt for you and I will not stop before the aristocratic prejudices that drive our society. I have the right to be happy." Amelie closes her eyes while the stubborn knight opens the door to leave and then he closes it with a dull thud. Never would have thought that a noble could fall in love with her. But perhaps it is just wrong. Maybe it's just intrigued by their different social situation. The king had called libertine so used to having any woman at his feet. His stubborn refusal may have attracted more than necessary but nothing more. From now on, not to suffer needlessly, should think about their mistake and forget this meeting. If only she had never met!

15.

"Hurry up we're late. I hate to get past guests as" The Marquis Pombery is stopped, standing in the middle of the room with a posture like a good soldier. He wears a black silk frock and a pink shirt. The pants dark gray finish with lace. Obviously, after joking remarks of his friend, has deliberately failed to wear the usual powdered wig curls. Collected the long blond hair in a queue with a black velvet ribbon. "Please do not get rage. I did not really want to take part in this pompous dinner of venison. As you know I hate to eat meat." "Of course I know the ladies love fish!" Pierre wears his green velvet jacket and you look in the mirror. The face is marked by fatigue more mental than physical. "Stop make fun of me! Otherwise, take your beloved club, which only God knows what you can serve, and make a dramatic entry into the apartments of the king "Charles, realizing he had gone too far with the jokes, sits in his chair by the window and watch Count dress. "Excuse me, is that I am a bit 'embarrassed. Usually these dinners Louis XV only invites close friends and allows only his closest servants to have access to his chambers. Indeed I thank you for allowing me to participate. The king would never have asked but thanks to our friendship." "From the stop, I was joking. I must admit that without your sunlight I would get bored to death here in court. Do you like these brown pants?" "I think they are perfect with the jacket which you wear." Pierre hated get help from the attendants to dress. The ritual felt too intimate to feel the eyes of another person pointed at him. But Charles was different. He already knew him from his first entrance into the palace. Their friendship became immediately so obvious that the king had given permission to the Marquis of living in an apartment near his friend. Before then went to court only for holidays or for audiences of kings. Yet his affection for the count did not depend on mere recognition but it was true and sincere. He considered that his brother never had. "Let's meet this evening boring!" "Don't exaggerate. You'll enjoy it more than you think!" He binds his hair with a green ribbon and he orders to the valet de chambre for stoking the fire. "Thanks Paul. I can't stand with the cold and this room is very humid for my taste." When passing through the Hall of Mirrors he encounters the countess Chambery who is walking with other noblewomen. "Good evening, Count, I see that you're heading to dinner the king. Congratulations on your jacket, it has a very hot color." She wearing a light dress that highlights her blond hair and big blue eyes. A man can hardly pass by without much notice it is its looks. Objectively the count is honored for the interest she feels towards him and that never fails to manifest. Many nobles would be in place, not only for the beauty of the girl but also for its favorable position toward the king. Whenever he finds in front of the Count tries to rethink all these advantages, but, as far as effort, can not prove anything more than a friendship. "How nice to see Mademoiselle Chambery. We were just going to the apartments of the king. What you do tonight?" "Oh, nothing exciting. We will go into the apartments of the queen listened to a concert piano. I hope to see you again tomorrow to make a healthy walk outdoors. "If time will allow more than willingly. Have a pleasant evening Countess." Pierre bows followed by Charles, who promptly moves to let the group of noble women in his wake. The rest of the journey continues in complete silence. After crossing the courtyard of the Bucks, climb the stairs covered with black and white tile with a beautiful wrought iron railing and gold. These rooms, defined small cabinets of kings, are known by a few noble because it is here that Louis XV was locked up for his private moments. Are not painted like the rest of the palace but covered with wood paneling with white stucco ceilings decorated in gold or light colors. Here the sovereign has the freedom to dispose of its real clothes to share with close friends banquets and speeches unrelated to strict court etiquette. Since the first flight of stairs he heard a deafening noise of voices and coarse laughter. Two attendants on either side of the entry call and ask them the following consideration opens the large wooden door inlaid with white floral pattern covered in gold. The wooden floor shines under the lights of candles. In the center a huge table set at will and illuminated with three large chandeliers. The guests are not many but the confusion is almost deafening. The king greets them by opening his arms in a friendly manner. "Welcome! Don't hesitate to serve you everything you want." The Marquis Pombery bows so awkward and the count returns the welcome with a smile. "Sire, we are very pleased to be your guests. A female voice behind them attracts their attention. The Marquise de Pompadour sits at the head, the only woman among many men addicted to the pleasure of food. "Count Lavois and Marquis Pombery but what a pleasure! Come sit at my sides, so you take care of myself in the midst of this pleasant confusion" With her joviality and enchants all the guests can follow the discussions typically male. The Marquis is enjoying like crazy. Just sit tight has been friends with a viscount by his side and began to speak without interruption. Pierre pretends to listen to the king, intent on making an account of his hunting today, but the thoughts fly elsewhere. "Count I ask you a question?" The voice of the Marchioness him back to reality. "Of course! There scruple, quietly spoken!" "Lately I have noticed more thoughtful fraternal affection I feel toward you lead me to worry. If I change your mood was fairly obvious when you met this young seamstress. I'm wrong? "Would you deny the obvious but the sweetness and kindness of the De Pompadour instill confidence so much that he decided to reveal his secret. He tells her what happened during the party at the Opera and feelings it produces. "I do not even recognize. I also had the audacity to introduce the boutique where she works... But she is more stubborn than she looks! "The

Marquise smiled and she hid her mouth with a napkin embroidered with silk in the real figures. "Let me do it! Only a woman can understand and try to convince another woman!" "I am grateful but I want the king to marry the Countess Chambery..." "This is a problem that will fix you. If I work to change his opinion might think that I have an interest to you. It does not seem a good idea... " At that moment Pierre looks down on a tray filled with oysters. "Serve the fish right? I always remember to make happy my dearest friends. Now you feel safer in trust me?" Surprised by this warm gesture he makes a big sigh before serving to let the waiter standing behind her.

16.

“Do you have some hot tea?" Annie is sitting on the bed between the old and curious patterns. "No thank you, after I finish this sleeve and I would just close your eyes until tomorrow morning." "But they are only eight o'clock. I wanted to talk a bit before sleeping." Since you returned from that famous business appointment at Versailles all you do is just stand and sewing her mouth shut. You send me an infinite sadness. Instead of being happy to make clothes for court." Amelie supports her work on the table in the back room and she stretch your arms up, yawning as she was a child. "I am apprehensive, afraid to make mistakes. This task is bigger than me and I do not feel up to the situation." Annie moves patterns and lies on its side leaning my chin with his elbow. "Come on, you know you're a good, indeed, an excellent seamstress otherwise why bother many courtiers come to town to get a suit when they have so many tailors and seamstresses available at court? Rather I think your problem is called Pierre Lavois "At the sound of that name is dropped on the bed like a dead weight. Raise your eyes to the ceiling, then closes them looking for the courage to tell her friend everything. "A girl of humble origin should not even think of a noble if not as his master or employer.

"Ugh! How boring you are! You are trying to hide something with these beautiful little words? But because yesterday the count was good out here at the door of the boutique?" Amelie turns suddenly assuming an expression of amazement. "But how do you know?" I was returning with fresh flowers when I saw a man tying his horse to the ring of our wall. When he removed the cap cloak I immediately recognized his face. I thought it best to do another round in the first quarter to break the eggs in the hamper!" She start playing nervously with a few locks of her hair rebels. "There's nothing to break because there is nothing but a simple knowledge." Ah, so I want to believe that he came to be when a suit may well be ordered to court and possibly not even to pay since we think his majesty." The circle tightens and he feels the sting the eyes too annoying to try to hide it. Burst into silent tears."He told me I needed to see me and that he was bewitched by my figure and my temper..." She takes a handkerchief from his bedside to blow his nose. As efforts are unable to stop crying. "Are you kidding? But how nice! Are not you happy?" "No, I'm absolutely delighted, indeed! This, if the truth would only worsen the situation. I'm just a seamstress and he is a noble!" Annie gets up and sits beside her. Put his arm around her waist and squeezed her with brotherly instinct. Then Amelia leaves her arms." Then why have you come up to here?" "Sometimes the rich are bored of their lives and want to experience new emotions. Maybe I'm a figure so different from those who attended every day by being attracted to but..." "For once in your life you believe in the words of others? You can always look at only the negative part of each event." She squeezes the handkerchief in her hands. "I will not deceive or daydreaming. Since I first saw my heart seems crazy." Annie takes her face and she looks straight into her eyes: "So you've already begun to suffer!"

"Will not you take me hunting tomorrow count?" The cold air and icy wind muffles the voice of the king, but not prevent Pierre heard the call that he hates more than any other. Any nobleman in his place would do somersaults to the request received but he hates killing animals of any kind. "Thank you Lord but I don't like hunting. I don't want to invent silly excuses not to go wrong in your eyes, I can not lie to me. I do not like not eating meat, I prefer the fish or vegetables. Excuse me, I would not be a good company or some help." Louis XV is back, he is enjoying with the perfect flowerbeds of the Orangerie. I heard him laugh and be certain when he turns to give him a pat on the back right. "I really like your frankness. I can say that about you I never had doubts. That is your respect towards me is not performed for something in return but because they really try. I have great confidence in you!" "Thanks, I'm honored!" He resumes walking slowly. Behind guards follow them at a safe distance. "If I did not trust so much of you I would have spent away from my dear

Madame de Pompadour!" The rest of the journey continued in silence. The wonderful ambience that relaxes the mind of Pierre for an hour can not think of his complicated emotional situation. Almost near the main entrance of the palace when the king made a sign to leave before guards leave them alone. A premonition makes its way into his mind. "Before getting in my private apartment..." He goes to his ear and he places a hand over her mouth to be sure of not being heard by the guards stopped at the entrance gate. "Which that we know in a few, including you." They feel that some noble women are watching them with curiosity. Then the king goes away and takes back his real attitude. "I'd be happy to hear you announce your engagement to the Countess Chambery. It 's a lovely girl, very beautiful and admired by the whole court. Its position can only strengthen your ". His forebodings were correct but instead of answering honestly hardly smiles and he remains silent. Do not mind but can not even be honest. A beautiful sound of wheels on the pavement of the square opposite the main entrance is to turn the two men. Only when the driver opens his door Pierre tightens the leather gloves that he has just removed. Amelie is pointing to the valets who take boxes. She doesn't turn, she narrows the cape and she shoulders erect start meeting with Madame de Pompadour. "I think that my dear Marquise needs (of) your help! And I'm sure you too will be curious to see her new clothes, right?" The problem is not to judge the performance of the new dressmaker but to support her eyes. And he hope that her anger may have dozed off.

18.

This time in going the entire route up to the apartments of Madame de Pompadour she tries to keep calm even though her legs were shaking so much that almost stumbling in the large marble staircase. The noble women who she meets along the way they look at her the more curious the first time, now they know who is.

The three attendants continue shipped so that she could not keep up. The architectural marvels of this palace is so much to the fascination not feel you have reached your destination. The same waitress the first time opens the big door and invited her to come making them the way to the long corridor. The Marquise is sitting at his desk busily writing a letter. Just see it leave the pen in its case and welcomes with open arms. "Hello dear! What a beautiful dress you wear." Amelie adapted one of her latest creations, a simple dress in ivory silk with turquoise lace in the sleeves and along the neckline of the bodice. Of course no panier that could hinder the natural development of her work. The hair left them loose without any adornment, ultimately she did not have to go to a dance and so she felt more at ease. "Good morning to you, Madame." She is excited at being embraced by a person as important. "You are so cute and very polite. You have a really pretty face and a smile so radiant!" "Thanks, I'm honored. You make me blush with these compliments, "The Marquise approaches to the table and she sits down. "But what do you say! You should blush, but delighted, if a man were to them to you. Please sit down." She motioned to a servant to lay the suitcase on the floor and hang the clothes hangers in the closet wrapped in white wood with gold designs, deliberately left open for the occasion. The waitress serving an hot chocolate with a tray full of delicious cakes of all colors. She start removing the paper from her creations suffered when she hears the door open. Not sure she just turns the sovereign who is approaching his beloved favorite. When she looks up the redness of a few minutes before regaining his face more clearly. The Count Lavois is kissing the hand of the Marquise and bowing before her. "Very pleased Mademoiselle Amelie. If you don't bother I am curious to see the results of your work." He sits down payment to De Pompadour and he crosses his legs. He wears a red velvet jacket and black trousers. Unlike many other nobles did not wear wigs but never ties his hair blacks, very bright, always with a ribbon to match the jacket. After showing clothes with an accurate description of the Marquise is absent in the room to go try one. "I hope not to have made a major disappointment in being entered into these rooms. But this is my duty to the sovereign." "It can disturb this is your home. I un'invitata. The count goes his forehead and he shakes his head. "Oh, start again with this nonsense. Always raised the walls where we could shoot them down. " Amelie is going to respond when entering the marquise with her dress in blue silk. Both the praise for its elegance. "Count I can ask a favor?" "Sure. Everything you want!" She looks and smiles sweetly as a sister. "You leave us alone? I need to talk to this wonderful creature. The famous dressmaker of Paris, and now of the royal family!" Only when she hears the door slam behind her, she began to tremble again. What makes her so agitated not only the fact of wanting to ask what this woman so powerful but also the news, coveted by Madame Rose, she has been selected as a seamstress in the king's favorite. "Don't make that face my dear. There looks nothing scary." She looks in the mirror and she takes the fan with turquoise ostrich feathers. Then she pretends to wave to her mouth to hide malicious. She turns and she nods to the waitress to take away the empty cups. Now they are completely alone. "How do you think to live here in Versailles? Or rather in the room next to my apartment?"

19.

After leaving the apartments of the Marquise De Pompadour, Pierre was thrown on the bed still dressed. He refused lunch and he fells asleep like a stone. Now in his sleep heavily knock on the door but he doesn't have the strength to rise. "I know you let me in!" Charles's voice brings him back to reality. He looks out the window and he sees that his relief is always day. The bell rings and let the valet to bring his friend. The Marquis comes with a stick adorned with a gold knob, a blue velvet coat and a white silk shirt full of lace. "Oh but you were sleeping with the dress? But that makes you distraught?" Pierre stands up slowly and he looks great in the mirror on the wall. "I will see you when you wake up!" He takes off his jacket handing the valet. Then the friend who looks in the meantime, as usual, he was settled quietly on the couch next to the bed. "You pretty but how you dress? There is a dance in the middle of the afternoon?" He puts the stick on the wall and then turns a mischievous look. "No, my dear, I have come to get you because I wanted to go for a walk in the park along with the Marquise and with some noblewomen of the court." Pierre removing the tape from his hair and he passes a hand to try to accommodate you. "You'll never change! As soon as you hear the name of a woman throws you like a beast on its prey. You are pathetic!" But really it’s your reputation as a heartbreaker and not mine." He drinks a champagne and hands him a glass even to the Marquis. "It must also have the class to court a woman. You are too bold!" He appears at the window and he sees a bunch of people who speak their own entry in the palace square. At the center he seems to see the small figure of the Marquise de Pompadour, almost hidden from others for his small stature. He had initially decided to refuse the invitation of his friend but knows he can not miss seeing one of his appeal. "So how long do you need to change you and honor of your company?" Tells footman in red velvet jacket that had until a few minutes before to leave and to help him. "I'm ready! Pass the red velvet ribbon at a table nearby." He binds her hair again and he came up with a firm step toward the door. Charles gets up and he picks up the stick. "Hey, but all this fury. Wait for me!" "Let's not fair to expect women! "In a moment I was out, the Marquis has the breath for running. "Here they are! Finally we were waiting!" The Marquise greets them and lets kiss the hand both. He sounds like a helpless child, wrapped in his woolen cape lined with fur. Yet she is the most powerful woman in all of France. The king's wife, paradoxically, have little voice and she lead a retired life. Among the noble women who accompany the notice Baroness and Countess Marie Tramèr Chambery. Begin to walk along the Grand Canal, Charles is positioned right in the middle of the group and women burdened to do more jokes can to attract their attention. The Marquise laughs, more for education for the real fun of his arguments. At one point trying to get a bit 'more backward than other approaches and that from that moment Pierre had followed silently and gently pulling the group. "I think I have done it." Count the turns a questioning look. "Excuse me, I don't understand you!" The dressmaker in Paris, Amelie. Will to live next to my apartment." For a moment his eyes light up then a doubt the axle. "But the first should have the consent of Madame Rose" Madame De Pompadour stops and tshe urns shooting. "Do you want to oppose to a decision of the king?" Certainly will not have the courage but Amelie is happy for the new life that awaits? A young girl who has always lived in a simple and far from comfort, may accept as an everyday life full of luxury and debauchery? "Monsieur Lavois you can come here a moment?" Baroness Tramèr calls him flirtatious attitude behind her Countess Chambery lance to her some glances of contempt. Pierre in his heart thanked her friend Marie, who takes away from this mess with innate elegance. He takes leave of the Marquise and he offers his arm to the baroness, while Charles awkwardly tries to comfort the countess.

20.

"I will not go!" Amelie cried incessantly for more than two hours. Madame Rose and Annie were trying to comfort her but without success. "Dear, a valet has left us a signed letter for you from Madame de Pompadour and from the king himself. Try to understand me, I can not oppose such a request. He is our sovereign. For me you're a big loss but you will remain in my service. Let me explain what I'm going to do. I will continue to give you a salary and you will continue to work for me. As customers will purchase all the courtiers who live in Versailles and then you will not be able to sew day and night, so Annie and I will do the rest. " Suddenly stop complaining like a spoiled child. "What a fool I am. I did not think the general economic advantage that I can get you. Excuse me Madame, I was hasty in my decision. Only now in retrospect I realize that you have won a place of honor at court." Annie covers gently. "That's great that I can come to visit you and finally to see this wonderful palace that everybody talks about!" "Girl all you do is think about the frivolities of life!" Madame Rose raises her voice to Annie but she amused smiles. The voltage of a few hours before it is fading and Amelie finds his usual smile. "Come on, get up! For tonight I offer you a dinner at my house. Ordered to cook all fish and a better way to collect chocolate cake and then tomorrow you will have plenty of time to pack your bags!"

21.

The dance last night was really boring, the Countess Chambery had never left him for a second. He could not break away from her because he felt the eyes of the king upon them. He invented a stupid excuse, a simple headache, to retire very soon. "You dont't bear the Countess, right?" The Baroness Marie Tramèrie approached him a few moments before he left the Hall of Mirrors. "My dear, if I continue to stay there close you will separate from the court. She is spoiled and mischievous, her close friendship with the king did her a security unbearable! And she is boring." Arrived at his apartment he was robbed in a hurry and then he was thrown on the bed like a dead weight. "Excuse me count Lavois the Marquise asks for you" The voice of the groom wakes him up permanently. "I get up immediately and I dress in a flash. I'm going to get her attention." He watchs the clock on the wall. The eleven of a normal Wednesday. On January 22, 1749. The commotion coming from the room next to the apartments of the De Pompadour curious but decides not to pry into even if the door is ajar. The waitress nods to enter, it immediately affects the silence that reigns within. "Sorry, but there is none?" The young girl looked at him shyly, then with the full red cheeks, find the courage to respond. "Madame will arrive in a few minutes, meanwhile told me to serve tea with pastries. "Yes, thanks. I have not had breakfast. " Before sitting looking at the mirror. In the rush he has worn the jacket which he normally uses to ride, as the same pants with matching leather boots. All in a shade of green undergrowth, as his mood somber. As soon as the tea is served pounces on the cakes on silver tray, remembering the night before he had not touched food. The sounds continue in the next room. He gets a book from the table of the Marquise. It has the leather cover, well bound and visibly used. Its pages are so faded as to make it more interesting. It's the "Histoire de France". Pierre is surprised by the choice of reading so busy and sometimes even boring for a woman. Then he smiles and he thinks that the marquise is not a woman like any other. She was erudite, kind, friendly and very curious about everything that surrounds her, from botany to architecture, literature and even switching to mathematics. And intent in these thoughts and completely abandoned the chair with a biscuit in one hand and the steaming cup on the table to his right when he hears footsteps. "Count sorry for the delay but I was helping my new station!" When Amelie sees behind the biscuit falls hand in astonishment. “Oh, that awkward" The Marquise smiled, her eyes makes him understand that she accomplished her difficult task. Now the dressmaker in Paris, her constant thought in recent weeks, has a new inhabitant of the palace. He can not believe his eyes. The king has been given to the request of his favorite but Madame Rose should not have prevented this decision. While the waitress tries to remove the remains of the biscuit, Pierre Amelie approaches and kisses her hand. "I am happy to see you!" "Thank you, very kind." The girl is so embarrassed by immediately turning their backs to look out the window. "How wonderful these gardens. Not to mention the fountains and the channel. It looks like a paradise!" " Count Lavois how about if instead of going to ride, saw your set, not accompanied our new tenants to visit the park?"

22.

They walk half an hour in complete silence. Both seem absorbed in their thoughts. When Amelia had revised him in the room of the Marquise, for the first time, she felt sympathy towards him. His figure, always so austere and studied, had appeared so funny with that biscuit on the other hand, fell awkwardly on the ground. Then his sportive dress made him more attractive and less highly placed than usual. So she perceived him a little closer than other times in which they were more clashes than encountered. Now, however, neither seemed to have the courage to break the obvious embarrassment. "I've never seen so large gardens and with a sublime architecture. A woman has more courage than a man. Thinking this, she decides to be the first to open his mouth. "It's a beautiful place to relax. In summer, the twittering of birds makes it almost a paradise!" They keep walking along the Grand Canal, under the curious eyes of other passersby. Amelie is wearing a red dress with no decoration or jewelry. The long curly dark hair fell over her shoulders. The cape that clasps in front of the chest against the cold winter wind, it is the same color as the dress. Surely the other nobles who cross the street not fail to notice her simplicity compared to where she is. "Do you like to ride?" The Count addresses this question while sitting on a stone bench in a grove side. He holds out a hand to help her sit beside him. "I regret that I never reveal mounted a horse in my entire life." He feels peer, so he pretends to admire the fountain in front of them. "A good opportunity to know you better. My Altoprato will be happy to accommodate you in the rump. Of course with me in command of the reins! "Amelie blushed with shame at the idea of being so close to him on a saddle. "But I do"t think that it's a good idea. I would only mess of your usual ride." "You're probably kidding? For me it will be a pleasure." She looks and she feels that she can trust him. His large dark eyes gave her security. The grate is made no word about their last meeting. With his calm and considerate behavior can not make her feel uncomfortable despite the simplicity of her attire. "So teach me to ride. Please!" The Count smiles, he gets up and he kneels. He takes both hands and looks straight into my eyes. "Get Ready! Tomorrow we start the lessons. In less than a month I will make you a true rider!"

23.

"Come on, come on! Get up from that chair. The king did not even deign of greeting me without you! "Charles shakes hands up and walk up and down the room, eager to head to the ball in the Hall of Mirrors. 'I just said, I must repeat once again? I do not want and I really sleep. " Pierre tries to hide the real reason his friend. It 'sure do not understand because ultimately you are having fun like crazy in any court understood the lady under the eyes. For him, however, the idea of being left alone in the midst of ducks available and engaged in futile discussions, the nausea. His thoughts turned to Amelia, locked in his room in isolation because they invited to a reception open only to nobles. "That damned seamstress gave you head! You have always been the most assiduous frequenter of salons and parties. Do not tell me that you love mica? "Better to keep up appearances and not to make public what is not yet clear in private. Call the valet and without answering his friend, wearing a jacket that is first. "Come on, hurry up and close that disgusting mouth!" From anger not directed another word the whole way. Walk like a thunderbolt sent Charles can hardly follow. The music envelops the long tunnel and lighted candles on the large crystal chandeliers create a beautiful play of colors with the immense ceiling frescoes. The many mirrors on the walls do the rest. For the occasion, the king did turn many lights along the Grand Canal so that anyone facing the big windows I can see the infinite length. It 's all shining, dresses, feathers, hair, jewelry. The eyes need a moment to focus before you get used to such splendor. "Good evening, Count Lavois. It 's a pleasure to see you. " Comes across in person just once would not want so much to see. Countess Juliette Chambery. 'It's always an honor to meet you! "She first looks around to make sure not to be heard, then sending a joke very risky. "It seems, lately just try to avoid me. We delight in the vicinity of Mile Tramèr more. I do not think that His Majesty will be very happy, "Pierre turns to search for his friend but the Marquis has already been lost in the crowd. "Sorry I do not understand what's wrong with sharing of healthy walks in the park with a friend of long standing? I do not see the malice, instead, you want to insinuate "In a split second you realize you have been too rude in response, but now the die is cast. "Indeed I take this opportunity to ask to speak briefly in private. Want to follow me? "The hands and arm are about to reach the terrace. The eyes of the Countess are all for him. It 's more than clear his hope of long-awaited marriage proposal. "You see I have no intention of getting married. Forgive the harsh reality but I do not usually pretend. I dont want to spend the rest of my life with someone who does not love just because it has an important heritage or because it is so dear to the sovereign. " "But I thought that you were attracted to me. It's guilty of that whore of the Tramèrie" Pierre, trying to calm her, he takes her hands and he looks straight into her eyes. She begins to cry and she looked down. "Don't try to interfere other people. I don't think having to repeat to me that the Baroness is a dear knowledge and nothing more. If I tried something deeper to her I would be already married. When I have a clear idea not to wait long to act. Rather than try to have more respect for yourself! How would you live next to a man that does not prove anything to you?" Just then Charles faces the window. "Sorry Pierre, but the king wanted to greet you." He leaves the hands of the countess and, with composure, he nods his friend to return. "Go ahead in, I'll be right!" With his handkerchief he tries to wipe the tears but Juliette leaves him with one click and she said:"You'll pay!"

24.

"Do you like these croissants?" Amelie eat slowly watching the hairdresser who is styled the Marquise. After waking up in the morning, as usual, she started to sew a yellow silk dress and had completely forgotten to eat breakfast. She kept looking at the four-poster bed where he stayed to make sure not to dream. Then, in a pause and another, she rose from his chair and she went to admire the magnificent gardens of Versailles. In any case, that environment was so nice to strike almost frightening. About eleven o'clock she heard a knock at his door, she initially thought that was the count but she remember sthat the appointment was for early afternoon. She was overlooking the maid of Madame de Pompadour and aviation invited to breakfast in his apartment. She knew he could not refuse but he felt embarrassed. The Marquise tasted a croissant in a hurry and now she let comb and dress in front of her. "Did you were bored last night?" “No, madame, absolutely. I was so sleepy that I fell asleep when lying on the bed." "It 's really a great disappointment for me not being able to attend the festivities but I will do everything possible to convince the king." The very idea makes her tremble with fear. "No! I pray I don’t feel up to it. I prefer to work and make a walk in the park. I don’t care to hang out, I am a simply dressmaker." “It does not mean that you're not a woman! Learn to ride then we'll talk." That confuses the sentence and her face has to portray this wonder beacause the Marquise starts to laugh. The hair behind her not to move the motions. "Yes, my dear the Count Lavois told me he wants to teach you how to ride an horse. And he is commendable on his part. I'm happy, that boy has a sweet heart despite the appearance of ice!"Amelie is unable to speak. She supports the cup with tea on the table and she stands up. "If you don't mind, I would go to my room to continue my work. There I am sewing a dress simple yet fine as silk used comes directly from the Indies." "You are a love. I trust you blindly! The materials used are of incomparable beauty. I'm so proud to have you in my service! You made my measurements and then what you want in complete freedom. I think you have taste to sell as well as talent."

25.

Altoprato is left to prepare for the ride, kick with impatience to make a good race between fields. Pierre Amelie helps to rise then he positioned in front. "Now clasp me strong. Don't afraid, my horse knows how to be fast but secure" His eyes scared the fun and softens at the same time. When half an hour before he knocked at her door he found busily sewing a dress for the Marquise. Her devotion to work was impressive. He could see immediately that she gave her joy and satisfaction. Then she got up to meet him and he for the first time, she was almost embarrassed. Her beauty is breathtaking. She could appear attractive with clothes humble and chaste. She had only a lace or lace gown, no panier, a green velvet. The hair had bound them in a high tail. "We look like brothers! We wear the same colors." She laughed at his joke. "At least the others will not notice us!" The air is very fresh and pleasant this afternoon. Pierre spurs Altoprato that starts immediately at a gallop, happy to give vent to his physical strength. Amelie felt sad life gently. After fifteen minutes Pierre pulling the reins firmly and he stops running. Amelie helps get that lands just trying to sit her hair all disheveled. He throws his cloak on the grass and invites her to sit on. "This place is an oasis of peace!" Her cheeks are flushed cold but her eyes sparkle with happiness. "It's a chance to live this earthly paradise. I love riding in this park." Before going to their appointment he had promised not to speak in respect of his statement took place in the boutique “La Belle Dame”. It was not yet the right time to tackle such a sensitive subject. The reassuring to see so friendly and kind to him. It was nevertheless a step forward. The rest of the way he discovered every day. "Get a horse every day?" "When the time permits me I like to give free rein to Altoprato. I consider him my most sincere confidant. I told to him everything that I love more." The animal calmly munching grass in front of them. "You can be sure of being understood and certainly never betrayed!" They smile together. Pierre inadvertently touches a hand. Instead of retreating Amelie shook her gently and she looks. He can not hold back and he strokes her face. She, to his amazement, not refuse his touch but she puts her hand on his. He still leans forward hesitantly and only when he realizes that is not her intention to withdraw, he kisses her.

26.

After a sleepless night Amelie can't concentrate at her work, her eyes burning and her hands shaking. She does nothing but she thinks about what it happened yesterday afternoon. The embarrassment to review the count is so great not having courage to set foot outside their room. She got up at six, as usual, and had breakfast in his room. The idea of having to answer a few questions more compromising the Marquise made her shiver. She decided to hide from anyone what happened. Her moment of weakness was not to become public domain. Watch the clock on the wall that marks the twelve already. She is near to get up and she calls the waitress when she hears voices in the corridor. One, that women seem too familiar to resist their curiosity. She opens the door and she surprises to be found in front of her Annie's arm of the Marquis Charles Pombery. She don't even notice her so committed to laugh. "Annie, what are you doing?" She just realizes she tries to take a more serious demeanor. "Hello. I found the Marquis as I climbed the stairs and offered to accompany me, so I had to disturb the servants!" "Very kind of you Monsieur Pombery. Now please excuse us we have to work!" She gestures to get her friend and she politely greets the Marquis. "But that wonderful room. What beautiful all the walls pink and this bed is a marvel." "Sit down now. I hardly need tell you what you have been shameless in accompanied by a man with no servants in tow. You went past the apartments of Madame de Pompadour if you had seen that figure would have done? Am I wrong or did you come to pick up the work you do in shops? "Annie continues to look around shows no remorse for what he has just done."Annie I'm talking to you! Listen to me or not?" "But how did you boring. Live in a fairytale, and you're doing so many unnecessary problems. " Every time I try to make them sound rumbling voice and finds himself no more angry than before. Should know by now. Her passion for the ephemeral and the appearance is beyond any sound principle. Perhaps it was this difference of views as to keep them together. She decided to surrender. "Want to have lunch with me?" "Yes, how nice! At least sample something different from the usual boring soup! "Amelie called the waitress who served the chicken with a delicious mayonnaise. All accompanied by a large portion of salad. When they get to dessert, a beautiful chocolate cake, she remains open-mouthed. "Oh but how much is covered with chocolate frosting. It 'a wonder for the eyes I dare not imagine the palate!" After sitting in front of the large work table and start looking for new fabrics and various commands to the Marquise. "You're full of work. But you have the time to play a bit?" "Annie here is not as you think. Or rather she is for the noble but I'm a seamstress and then live as such. Labor and the evening I go to bed very early. I do not go to parties or receptions do not have a title that introduced me to court." "But the count Lavois not take you with him?" She looks shocked by this question. "How can you go against the laws and real then I'm not his girlfriend. But what's got your head? He's just trying to teach me to ride, because I've never done before." Annie rises and she falls on her bed. "From what Charles told me not're indifferent! He says he has known since you try to desert any receipt just to be with you." Amelie looks down on their hands, without realizing it, are pressing hard a piece of fine silk. "Even so, at this age do not believe in fairy tales anymore."

27.

"I find it a fabulous idea? The King can't resist, after all I am who play and therefore I can choose my audience!" The Marquise had decided to invite her Amelie provides evening of Moliere's Tartuffe. "I am grateful. I will convince a company because she is very private." "I know. But I regret that she is locked in her room every night. It 's so young to a little entertainment.". Pierre sighs and he stands up. "Thank you Madame. I don't know how to thank you for what you are doing for me." "I know what it means to love and think of not being able to crown your dream. I was lucky, the king asked me to follow him and I won everything which I wanted. Unfortunately I have to settle for sharing him with other women, not only with his wife. Combining the charm of sovereign few can resist. If I told you that I love the man and not the position that he held me all laugh in the face. But you can be confident that this is the truth. I learned to live with the pain because of his constant betrayals, however, it's that I always return." The revelation of the unexpected and surprising glimpse of the most suffering of a woman smiling and joyful. Only then did she realize how hard it is to hide behind a happiness sometimes nonexistent. "This is my biggest fear. The idea that others can judge our report as an opportunity for social climbing. And this reason stop my heart." The Marquise, after the painful confession, regaining his usual smile. "You know sometimes just very little to reassure a woman. Ignore any bad comment in her presence. Let her understand that the opinions of others are not important for you. And you stay near her as possible. "

28.

He had initially decided not to go to recite of the marquise because she would feel like a fish out of water. She had all eyes on him. Then he thought about all the kindness she had reserved for her since her arrival. He could not refuse his invitation. Much less this kind of invitation, it was the play his greatest passion. "You are wonderful Amelie. Look like a goddess! "He can not hide his blushes after such praise. "You too are very elegant Count. This coat is made of green velvet extremely valuable." "You can not not examine every tissue that has passed before his eyes. Your work will also influence your moments of leisure." "But my job for me is already a delightful entertainment!" He provides for the last time in the large mirror on the wall. She wears a pink silk dress with an antique lace collar edged with white sleeves, long up to the elbows. The rebellious hair was dressed by a maid in a soft bun that has been affixed a few feathers in the color of the dress. On this occasion he chose to add the skirt to the basket. Even if you can not feel at ease so that you know will be a little easier to blend in with the small crowd. Indeed, the Marquise de Pompadour was used to send people to her loved ones because many of the most noble of her neighbors were involved in the drama itself. "Shall we go? Lean on my arm and try to always smile even when you do not want any. This is the world of appearance and essence" Amelie is a great breath and closes his eyes for a moment. Then, confident, relies on Count Lavois. When out of his room they encounter another couple going through the corridor just in that moment. "Annie?

What are you doing here?" "I came for see to recite the marquise. Not happy at least spend some 'time together?" The Marquis Pombery the bows continuing to support the girl's hand. "Good evening, dear! We want to hurry? Otherwise, although the closest to the apartments of De Pompadour we still reach for last. " The two they walk quickly past them. Amelie turns and looks at Pierre's eyes in disbelief. "It's been to invite Charles. Ah, of course, under the request of the Marquise. When he learned that Annie had come to visit you to collect labor thought you might like to spend free time again with your old friend." Why the rest of France think so badly about a woman as sensitive and generous?

29.

The evening was spent in harmony and lightheartedness. Amelie received much praise and some nobles laid their eyes on her. Annie was sitting next to Marquis arousing curiosity among the other guests. But Pierre, since their arrival in the apartments of the Marquise, he had felt so insistent observed. Only during the intermission of the performance he turned and seen the countess Chambery, who was sitting just two rows behind them and she was watching them. To try to avoid bad gossip, something almost impossible, she had approached. She had refused his hand and looking around with his usual flirtatious to him said a word. "I didn't know that you liked to spend time with the cheesy seamstresses. As wearing sumptuous clothes are always silly commoners. He didn't know whether to answer or ignore the bad joke. Her smile was directed to Amelia and her dear friend, the Marquis Pombery. Now, just finished the recitation, were walking in the Orangerie, lit by candles many suggestive. Cradled by the night breeze embraced gather to admire the beautiful flower beds. Squeezed against his chest then when he realizes his abandonment nice, kisses her passionately. A long and intense kiss. Clumsy attempts to regain control of herself and starts playing with a feather of his hair. Pierre, however, continues to look with admiration. "I wonder what he thought of me Countess Chambery when he saw me among the guests of Madame?" Pierre stopped abruptly and leaves his hand. "Why are you worried about his opinion?" She takes a step back as frightened by the effects of the application you have just made. "No, or rather not much that is our only customer. I know for some time and I know he is very fond of Madame Rose. It is a very demanding girl in the choice of fabrics and yet just enough to be admired. It's so beautiful!" "Yes Very pretty but so empty." Amelie sits on a stone bench and she shakes his woolen cape. "Why do you say so?" She wants to tell the whole truth. But think of not being able to do, she would refuse to continue their relationship soon blossomed. And Pierre just want to turn this into something more tender feeling deep. He has became clear just comparing the two women this evening. Come what may. Also give up his position at court. But it must at all costs. "Yes I know quite well because it is assiduous goers living rooms, receptions, dances and the most fashionable can move from Versailles. It 's impossible not to meet these events. But knowledge is like many others." “Oh, maybe it was pushed over due. Claiming that knowledge is like the others is very hazardous. Just because Amelie will still working relationship with her. Juliette, if I remember correctly, had sworn revenge.”

30.

"You were very good last night. I was enchanted by your talent!" Madame de Pompadour is sipping hot chocolate, she looks very tired but obviously satisfied. "How nice that you Amelie. I must confess to be very happy to have you invited. You were so smart as to turn the head of many men. One in particular. The Count Lavois had eyes only for you." "Oh, please, I am not to his height." The Marquise relax on the chaise longue in front of the window holding a croissant stuffed with cream." Even I was at the height of Louis XV. But, unlike you, I never post the problem, or at least I tried to remove him from my head. Otherwise I would never come down to here. Do you have a low opinion of yourself. Without that you can not get very far." Amelie observes the gardens of the park, the horizon dark clouds are threatening an imminent storm. "Excuse me if they are sincere but I will not get anywhere. Or rather, I'm fine here as a seamstress but I have other demands in life, I've already accomplished a lot, some people are worse off than me." "I know. Unfortunately I know very well. But I meant in a man's heart. Without the necessary trust and confidence in ourselves we do not breach any heart. Believe me! Even in the most humble" marvels at the unexpected council of the Marquise but he knows that she has so much character to put into practice. Or perhaps not want to have a future in the sumptuous palace so far from his idea of happiness.

From an early age had only dreamed of a small house and a man beside her could give her security and love. "You are right. I'll try to love me and treat my best aspect. For me it is already a big sacrifice." The Marquise reclined her head on the chaise longue and she closes her eyes. "Maybe it becomes a pleasure!"

31.

"Amelie are you in the room?" A few minutes is knocking on his door but no one answers, not even the maid. "Hello, I've been looking for?" She turns and she sees her reach from the apartments of the Marquise. Wearing a bright turquoise dress that highlights her dark hair and is in pleasant contrast with the cloudy sky this morning. "Yes! Sorry but I had come to invite you to lunch in my apartment. " Does not reply simply smile and then to look down. "I thought for a carefree picnics in the country but the weather forced me to leave

Altoprato barns. But I ordered the waiters brought to exquisite seafood. " He takes her chin and forces her to look into his eyes. "You can’t say no. I will talk a bit with you calmly." "What I think people will get into your apartment?" Pierre realizes his flushed at the thought of being judged." At Versailles there are always so many scandals to talk about that may not even notice it! And then you are a seamstress could give me a dress. Do not see anything strange." He rests his hand on the door of his room. "Okay, you convinced me. But just because you ordered the fish. I'm going mad." "Look what a coincidence, well I love him more than the flesh." Enter the room to inform the maid's absence, then is led with evident embarrassment. For every person we meet again lowers his gaze. Only when the valet to welcome them seems to breathe a sigh of relief. Just enter the anteroom, where a waiter is running out of the table, start off a stormy time. Pierre nods to light all the candles and add more wood to fireplaces, the gray sky made the atmosphere almost night. The chair moves the pile to make it accommodate and serve champagne as an aperitif. "No, thanks. But I'm not very accustomed to drinking alcohol. Prefer water!" "I can't find any fault. You are perfection in person!" "Why do you say that?" "You don't drink, you don't play, you have no vanity in dress either... " "I am a normal person. Fail to be different." "You are so intimidated by anyone blameless before you! Why not try to leave you a little 'go and live life day by day?" He regrets having said it, but at the same time that he feels a weight lifted. And to his amazement, Amelia seems to have offended. "I had already noticed that my behavior was not suitable to the place where I live now but are not very good at pretending." Pierre put your hands on the table as to eliminate any distance between them. I am face to face, only the large candle, gold hidden their full view of each other. The shift from one side completely removing every obstacle. Then order the waiter to start serving lunch. Outside, the raging storm of rain beating on the big glass windows. Peace of the room contrasts with the storm outside. Tasted in silence salad garnished with shrimp and boiled eggs. Amelie seems to be satisfied and more relaxed than before. Every time I look up and smile. "Oh it seems to me to dream. This dish was so simple to be delicious. " Wait till you taste the rest." The waiter approaches with two large lobsters are decorated with the mayonnaise. "Conte have exaggerated! This is a true delicacy. "So this magnitude together with this delicious white wine. Everything will become a stronger flavor. Seeing drink makes him smile. Fear of alcohol makes you squint when the glass door near the nose. But after just two sips seems more supple. "You see this is my dream." "Eating fish in a manner so blatant?" Pierre laughs just used the word understands that she has finally decided to break down some of his wall. "No. But for those who have taken me? I do not spend my life drinking and eating ..." Otherwise, the physical good that you'd found a really bad end, and with him all the eyes of every sentimental lady who is coming!" "Perhaps you are jealous?" No... no. Why should I be?"

The Count decides not to go ahead with his speech but to resume the interrupted another. Can not disclose that he, however, is bothered by the looks of appreciation of others. "My real dream is to produce wine. My father has a beautiful property in Provence. There are several hectares of land planted with vines just that almost squandered his entire fortune to the game and after his death has left me only to pay debts. Amelie wipes her lips with a napkin while watching him in disbelief. "What a disappointment! I heard that those lands are beautiful, always with a pleasant climate and very peculiar villages." The sorrow for the memory of their land makes him sad but tries to hide the pain continued his story. "I love living here in court. I wear a mask that is designed around a table. I created a character to attract the sympathies of the king. A lover of good life and fashion. This is what I appear to others but inside I fight every day a struggle to not bring out my true self. " "And why is such a torture on you?" "That was the only way to bring a bit of money in my funds to renovate the castle and his lands. I would like to start making wine, and retire there forever with no problems on how to dress or present myself as a receipt. "Why do I mention this? As I understand it is your intimate secret." Pierre holds out his hand and helped her up. He takes her face and he stares into his eyes. "Would you help me achieve this dream?" She steps back and she turns to the window. "What kind of proposal is this?" He is coming in small steps and he surrounds the life. "Read it as you like. Maybe a marriage proposal... "As soon as he turns and he kisses her forehead gently. She leaves him indulging in his arms and he is near to kiss her lips ... "Pierre I know who you're here, let me in! I must tell you something very important!"

32.

Perhaps due to his dialogue with the Marquise de Pompadour she was finally able to let go. If Charles had not knocked on the damn door she would even dare to go beyond a simple kiss. She must recognize that the presence of the Count Lavois shook her legs and warmed her heart. She could not resist. She had only heard his voice to melt like ice in the sun. When looked at him was lost in her large dark eyes. "Annie! Are you new here? And with the Marquis Pombery?"She was shocked looking at the friend who enter in the apartment at the hands of Charles. "I see you, my friend, you are in good company." The Marquis sits in a velvet chair and, after taking a crystal glass from the table, he drink a white wine. "Charles explain to me what happens? What are you doing around Versailles with Annie?" "This is the news that I wanted to give you. Actually we wanted to give you. Or rather, at this point, I can tell you." He stands up to his feet and he draws Annie though. He kisses her forehead and then he embrice her. "We're getting married!" Amelie cann't believe to her ears. The radiant smiles at her friend waiting for her reaction. She can not utter a word and she began to do her voice trembled. "But Madame Rose? Who will take your place?" The girl turns a look of disappointment. "Instead of thinking just cheer for me at work?" She feels anger breathtaking. Shaking their fists at her sides. "I look at the facts. You can't leave overnight your job so demanding as ours." Annie turns red in the face, she comes to her moving her hands in the air. "But you believe to be genuine and perfect to you? Madame Rose has already hired a girl who works in the field for many years. Did you know everything before you and did not the stories you're doing! You must hug me and wish me good luck. But you're not able to see the happiness, but only the duty in any situation." In one day, she received more accusations of a spoiled child. She realizes that she has exaggerated. "I'm sorry. You're right they are a boring old maid who doesn't believe in fairy tales." The covers with strength and she begins to cry. The two men looked incredulous. Then Charles abandons his glass on the table and he puts his hand on the shoulder of the count. "And also you here alone and forlorn, with a laid table, I told lies...." "Sorry but I must return to work. Annie, if I want to deliver to the patterns. I will take you in the room. Charles See you later!" The Marquis kisses her hand and salutes. Pierre, however, smiles at her tenderly. Their speech may be taken at another time.

33.

"Here, I have been waiting for you!" Amelie is in front of her door near the Countess Chambery. "Good evening, can I help you?" Juliette observes her from head to toe then she shifts her attention to Annie. "I need to talk privately. I don't need any clothes." The tone is austere and authoritarian, not to mention at least smile. "If you wait five minutes I leave to my work to my colleague and I am with you." "I hope that the wait is longer than had." Amelie is baffled by this hostile behavior, Juliette as assiduous customer of "La Belle

Dame", had always turned so gentle and kind. "Don't worry. Sit on the couch. I'll be right!" Annie leaves the room and the Countess in the adjacent lounge. "What ever will you?" "Annie I dont know for that reason, but she doesn't seem very happy to see me." After taking the patterns to achieve the girl hugs and kisses. "We see these days." "I'm happy for you. Charles is a nice person. Sometimes he may seem superficial, but I know his heart is much more noble title he wears. Will take care of you." "Thank you, Amelie! I recommend you do not stray from the count .. " Annie leaves the sentence open on purpose, the winking and she closes the door behind her. She accommodates her hair, she drinks a bit of water and she is ready for the mysterious meeting. The countess is inspecting every inch of the room where is located the workbench. "I thought we had an apartment for a bit bigger, but I see with pleasure that the king had common sense! I think it's already a scandal that a simple dressmaker living next to the favorite, but ultimately, she is she who wanted it to court." The hatred that emits the tone of his voice gives way stucco Amelie by failing to respond. She decides to act with sensitivity. "Do you want a tea with pastries?" “No. Let's go on." She start walking up and down in the room, she never removes her eyes off her. "What do you think that I'm blind? You came to Versailles to ruin my engagement?" With all her good will and for those seeking to commit she can’t understand what it refers Juliette. "Excuse me but I can’t follow you." "Do you even think that I am a stupid person? But good! You are just leaving the room of my future husband, you dined with him, do you see in his presence to the performances of the Marchioness and go riding together. Did not seem so drab when working in the shop of Madame Rose. What are you trying to do? Want to try to join the ranks of the nobility?" She is dropped on the chair and she runs her hand over her forehead. How could she know that Pierre was engaged to the Countess? That stupid to believe him. He just wanted to make fun of a poor woman of love and inexperienced stranger to luxury and good living. What must have been comical to him. "I ... I don't know that Pierre was your boyfriend." "How strange! King only wants our marriage. Otherwise it will drive out of the palace." She grab a cup of tea and she sips a sweet shot well to avoid fainting. "I really believe you among us there is only friendship and nothing more." "If you are really her friend then leave it alone! More and more your company will stay in the sovereign will ignore it. You will be his undoing. Without waiting for a reply, the Countess opens the door and she slammed behind her. Thunder startles Amelie. she gets to watch the storm of rain continues to lash the windows and she started to cry.

34.

Annie had informed him of the visit of Juliette. Pierre was unable to sit in his apartment, fearing the worst, had hastily directed toward the chamber Amelie. She had not opened and had not searched for more days. At a distance of one week did not know what to think or what to do to approach her. He knows that every morning he has breakfast with the Marquise, but lacks the courage to present himself for fear of a refusal. Could not stand in front of Madame de Pompadour. Is walking in solitude in the park when you hear a female voice call. Baroness Tramèrie smiles and, after greeting the other noblewomen, she comes close. "Good evening, Count Lavois, how are you? You don’t have a good wax." “I don’t feel very well. I think that I got a bit of influence." Marie was not convinced, she seems determined to get to the bottom. "You have neither nose nor reddened eyes moist. The heart does tricks?" Pierre stops and he looks startled by that insight. Not often, even try to wander with our eyes but she knows that her friend hit the mark. "That girl there has just changed. Better. Seem more human and less calculated. "Why do you say that?" "Have you already forgotten what was there between us? Your eyes have no more secrets now. I learned as a friend and I want the better thing for you, therefore, I want your happiness. Amelie can give you the peace which you need! I saw the other night at the recital, you seemed perfect together." Continue to hide their feelings he would be incomprehensible and childish. For the first time in his life he lets go to the most intimate secrets and he tells everything that had happened to the Baroness. Sitting on a bench he spend a good deal now. "Why not ask for help to the Marquise de Pompadour? You will convince her." "I don't want to do it. She has already helped me once and I can't take other advantage from her availability." Marie takes the one hand and she leads to her cheek. Her is a gesture of affection which has nothing of malicious. "Do you want me to talk me?" He tried to refuse but he knows that not have many other choices. You continue to avoid it. "Why not?"

35.

"Girl if you keep eating so little you'll end up all bones become your burden." Madame de Pompadour was looking for some minutes. She failed to get the appetite and ultimately always a non-existent migraine while pretending to decline croissants and pastries that she offered each morning. "I'm not very hungry. I spend all my day at work, I don't need a lot of energy." "Exactly. What has happened to the rides with the Count Lavois? I don't have more appointed." She puts the spoon and she remains silent for a moment, then she decides to tell her the truth. "I don't want to see him. I didn't know that he was engaged with the Countess Chambery. I don't want to ruin the lives of anyone. I have not the law." "Boyfriend? Who did she tell to you?" "Yes, she came into my room and she told me that the king has already planned their marriage..." The Marquise gets up and she opens the cabinet to decide what dress to wear. "And did you thought? The king treats it as an ideal wife for Pierre, but that does not mean that he is in love with her." Amelie shows a red satin dress then she help spread it on the couch. "From what I understand if you decide not to marry could lose its position of prestige here in court." "I told him several times in deciding to tell the truth to Louis. I can hardly believe it but it seems that Pierre doesn't have the courage to do it." The waitress peeps through the door. "Excuse me Mademoiselle Amelie the Baroness Tramèrie asks to be able to talk." The Marquise began laughing heartily. "I think that is acting as a messenger of your dear count. Receive her and listen carefully. No more than you know Monsieur Lavois."

36.

He can't still seems a schoolboy novice. Since the Baroness Tramèrie was directed to the chamber of Amelie he goes back and forth to his apartment. The servants look at him puzzled but amused. Recently they found a man much more frail and less attentive to the label. Sometimes he comes out without even looking in the mirror when the first spent hours in the choice of clothes to wear. The clock strikes five and still no news. To avoid going crazy waiting, he decides to visit Charles. He is surprised to find him in the company of a distinguished and well-dressed man standing near the desk. The marquis, however, is seated and is holding up his head with his hands. "What happened?" When he raises his face to greet discovers that he is crying. "My father died." Pierre forces him to stand up and embraces him with affection. "I'm sorry. Why don't you call me?" He hands him his handkerchief. "If I'd known that I was not well back home. I feel so guilty. I was here to enjoy between dances and receptions, and he, instead..." "How did you know? Provence is so close. You must not take on guilt that you have not." The man behind them, clearing his throat as if to remind his presence. "Oh, sorry. This is Monsieur Larray our lawyer." After the presentations ceremony, Charles sits back at his desk. "Now do you give your required to follow and take possession. What do you think to do?" "I had already decided to Annie. We are getting married and going to live in my villa in Nice. Enough of Versailles." He feels a pang, a friend showed him a lot more character. As soon as he met his soul mate has given up everything else. He has not been afraid to declare his plans to the king and losing his place at court. “Pierre owe me a favor very delicate. You can bring a lawyer from Amelie?" "Sure. What we covered her with all this?" "Stay in the room during their meeting, and then we'll talk."

37.

"You should talk to him. Or at least listen to what he had to say. How could you trust the Countess Chambery?" Amelie played nervously with a fold of her dress. After a few hours talking with Baroness Tramèrie in her mind begins to dawn on the idea of having the wrong behavior. She never opened the account when, on several occasions, she presented herself at her door asking only to listen. "You have right. But how could I think otherwise? I know Pierre only since two months. Once too small to not have any doubt about his promises." The Baroness wipes his mouth with a napkin and pushes the plate with dessert almost intact. "Maybe I am heartened to know that he never made any proposal. He never said a woman and if he did it with you is more commendable. You are a seamstress, you do not have titles, so what would be in scope at your side? Nothing. This can only be love. " Was filled with an uncontrollable desire to throw open the door and head to race to the apartment but try to restrain the Earl. When Marie is gone will consider his future moves to be forgiven. It 's so taken by his thoughts did not observe that the maid is calling. "Sorry but there Mademoiselle Count Lavois Larray and a lawyer wanting to talk." Baroness gets up, takes his gloves and heads towards the exit. "It seems that I am coming to visit you in your most gratifying moment. If our conversation is served in something, please do not continue to deny you happiness. " Just clashes with Pierre Marie exchange a furtive glance of understanding. What little is enough to make her understand that he was just asking him to speak. Sign fearful in the sitting room followed by a tall gentleman, of a certain age and gruff-looking. "Excuse me but the lawyer Amelie Larray have to tell you some things, and Charles asked me to accompany him... and if you please assist. "Please sit Pierre and sorry if I was not the company recently. The mere fact of having called him by name, as he had never done until now, shortens the distance between them. In a moment can apologize for the eyes of Count show that he appreciated that choice. "Please sit down. Can I offer you some tea? "Call the waitress and asked her to clear the table quickly and take tea with lots of pastries. The lawyer is standing as concerned about what to announce. "The Marquis Paul Pombery died yesterday at his villa in Nice." Amelie turns to the Count with shining eyes. "Oh what a bad news for Charles." "Yes Also because he saw him some time." "Excuse me Mr but I'm not here just for this! Your mother named Yvonne and a young age had served in the Marquis. Then his wife had made her drive because she had discovered the relationship with her husband. Relationship from which you are born you, Mademoiselle Amelie!" Pierre has time to hold her while it seems faint. The spreads on the couch and he gets the salts by a footman. Knowledge, but resumed immediately begins to cry silently. "Why I have not heard before? I have known my father. I thought that he was dead... " "I'm sorry but the Marquis wanted to silence all talk and evil had left written after his death you would have had to divide the inheritance with Monsieur Charles, your brother." After years of suffering and sacrifices she discovers that the rich feel uncomfortable. It's like having to change skin. The count seems shocked by the news but at the same time happy. He is near to open his mouth again when they hear a knock at the door. Charles enters his eyes red from weeping, spreading his arms and he shakes Amelie. "I didn't have a sister but I'm so glad you both! I am honored to share the property of our father with a person so sincere." "No! I don't want anything. And it's right that you to continue your legacy of our father .. or better." "This never! I am a straight man and if that was his desire is also my" The voice is firm and determined. "Okay. Then I want a small part to help my fiance, the Count Lavois present here, to renovate his villa in Provence and his related land to cultivate." Pierre takes her up and he twirls her in the air. "We're ready for a new life!" Now the king have little to say. You are not a simple dressmaker, but the Marquise Amelie Pombery. In any case, the court didn't have thoughts of most importance, their lives will be much more quiet in the south of France.

EPILOGUE

September 1749

Vence. (Provence) Altoprato Castle.

"Altoprato Go, go that Pierre is waiting for us!" Now riding a tube, Amelie, spent much of his free time riding the impetuous black stallion. The rest of the day she followed the Count to help the laborers in the vineyards in the grape harvest. She could not be happier. She still enjoy sewing clothes for some customers who, fortunately, were not as demanding as the court ladies. From a distance you can see the castle, surrounded by green hills. In recent months, they tried to restructure it to better and so they been forced to shift their wedding date from August to November. At least they would enjoyed their first day of harvest and so would uncork a bottle of their wine. The peasants shake hands as he passed, Pierre, among them the mention of going to the castle. On arrival Charles sees Annie's hand that are waiting under the large olive tree garden in front of the stables. "What kind of boy you've become?" She throws off Altoprato and she embraces her friend and brother. "What a nice surprise! What brings you here?" "We were invited Pierre to help the harvest." "Oh, that's why he asked the maid to prepare the guest room. I did a really nice gift!" The way towards the door of the castle when they reached the count. Charles starts almost crying from happiness. But the surprises are not over. A carriage travels slowly up the dirt, dust that makes up its outline barely visible. It does not seem in good condition, the wheels creak and the driver is wearing shabby clothes. Only when it stops in the courtyard of the castle door opens suddenly. The result is a woman of small stature, hidden by a large hat covered with feathers. Amelie has heart sank when he smiles and takes it off for four friends who watch open-mouthed. "What? You are not happy to see me? "The Marquise de Pompadour smiles beaming. "Oh but this is the happiest day of my life!" "Baby don't look that way because I knew nothing. I can assure you." 'It's true! It was I who decided to come, of course I have tried to travel as unknown. Can you imagine if in these roads are presented a royal carriage?" We all laughed. "We would like to prepare the best room. It will not be as Versailles but you will enjoy a beautiful view." When she left the palace she felt relieved that we no longer get lost in futile discussions and receptions boring but left my heart in this unique park. "This castle is very beautiful and also the place is so relaxing." Winking in Amelia and takes his arm. Leave behind the others and head to the garden. "How could I miss your first grape harvest?"

Versailles

in the time of the king Louis XV

Paris Opera.
Where were often organized dances and parties throughout the French nobility.

The King Louis XV

(Versailles 15.2.1710-10.5.1774).

The great Hall of Mirrors.

Madame de Pompadour
(Paris 29.12.1721-Versailles
15.4.1721).

Particular woman's dress at the time of Louis XV.

If you have any criticism, positive or negative, I will look you on my blog and my website:

http://www.samilla.wordpress.com

http://www.catastinisamanta.ilcannocchiale.it

The characters in this book are pure fiction. As for Louis XV and Madame de Pompadour my interpretation was purely free even if documented.

www.ingramcontent.com/pod-product-compliance
Ingram Content Group UK Ltd.
Pitfield, Milton Keynes, MK11 3LW, UK
UKHW020128250726
13967UKWH00002B/539

9 781445 764566